Who Would You Choose?

Books by J. M. Bronston

A PURRFECT ROMANCE

HER WINNING WAYS

SUMMER ON THE CAPE

A COWBOY'S LOVE

WHO DO YOU LOVE?

WHO WOULD YOU CHOOSE?

Published by Kensington Publishing Corporation

Who Would You Choose?

J. M. Bronston

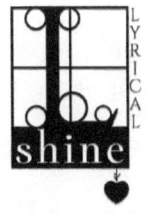

LYRICAL SHINE
Kensington Publishing Corp.
www.kensingtonbooks.com

LYRICAL SHINE BOOKS are published by

Kensington Publishing Corp.
119 West 40th Street
New York, NY 10018

All Kensington titles, imprints, and distributed lines are available at special quantity discounts for bulk purchases for sales promotion, premiums, fund-raising, educational, or institutional use.

Special book excerpts or customized printings can also be created to fit specific needs. For details, write or phone the office of the Kensington Sales Manager: Kensington Publishing Corp., 119 West 40th Street, New York, NY 10018. Attn. Sales Department. Phone: 1-800-221-2647.

Lyrical Shine and Lyrical Shine logo Reg. U.S. Pat. & TM Off.

First Electronic Edition: November 2018
eISBN-13: 978-1-5161-0322-5
eISBN-10: 1-5161-0322-X

First Print Edition: November 2018
ISBN-13: 978-1-5161-0323-2
ISBN-10: 1-5161-0323-8

Printed in the United States of America

ACKNOWLEDGMENTS

The writing of this book has been a happy jaunt down memory lane. But alas, sometimes memory fails. I am therefore much indebted to my friend Diny Tecker, and to her friend Elly Ameling, whose excellent memories along with their sensitivity to traditional culture and social behavior provided invaluable guidance in portraying a landmark Viennese coffee house.

I also much appreciate the assistance of Christian Ebener, Deputy Director at the Austrian Cultural Center in New York City, who was generous in sharing with me information concerning traditional and contemporary Viennese etiquette in such matters as forms of address and the use of visiting cards.

My thanks, too, to Scott Cullen, the General Manager at the Broadwalk Cafe in London's Kensington Gardens, who helped me set that scene.

Nydia Providence, M.D. set aside time out of her very busy schedule to sit with me and answer all my medical questions. This is my sincerest "thank you" to her.

As always, I am fortunate in having John Scognamilio and his colleagues at Kensington Books as my editing team. They save me from so many errors and I am profoundly grateful.

Liza Fleissig, my agent, and Ginger Harris along with everyone at the Liza Royce Agency keep my eye on the prize. They provide incredible energy and support. What would I do without you?

And the four people who are my treasures – Annie, Mary, Margaret and Nick. Thank you just for being.

Chapter One

"When does his plane get in?"

"Not till three."

"And he's coming here first thing?"

"Yes. He should be here by four."

"And that's actually what he said?"

"Yes, Marge. That's actually what he said. He did the shoot. He didn't like the pictures. He's not sending them in." Frieda was poised near the door, hoping to get out of there as quickly as possible.

"He knows the issue closes in less than two weeks, doesn't he?"

"I'm sorry, Marge."

Marge closed her eyes briefly, took a single deep breath and smiled a small, patient smile. This, too, could be managed. Then she spoke very quietly to her assistant, Frieda Cox.

"He's a genius." She pursed her lips ever so slightly. "Piero Massione is a photographic genius. But he must be almost seventy by now, and the older he gets, the more he becomes a prima donna. Give me twenty minutes with him as soon as he arrives. We'll work it out." She stood up and slipped into her jacket. A collarless linen from Oscar de la Renta—perfect for the soft breeze of this early September morning. And she got her sunglasses out of her handbag. The sunglasses were from Celine. The bag from Chloé. She glanced at the Mark Cross calendar on her desk—a gift from Jerry Germaine. Jerry was Marge's long-time boyfriend. "I'm on my way to that retailers' meeting. Then I'll be at the Bryant Park for lunch, meeting Bridey Berrigan to talk about her next food column."

"Yes, Marge."

"And call Jerry. Tell him yes, I can meet him at seven for dinner. At Galba's."

And she was out of the office and down the hall to the elevator.

"Yes, Marge," Frieda called after her. And to the empty air, she whispered, "Marge Webster handles disasters like they were soap bubbles."

* * * *

It was just too good a day not to be outside in the sun. The retailers' meeting had gone really well and ended early with smiles all around. She was ahead of schedule for her lunch appointment and the city was inviting her to come out and breathe a little.

"Luke. Stop the car." She looked at her watch—a gift from Hermès—and said, "I have some time. I'm going to walk from here. You go on to the restaurant and wait for me till it's time to go back to the office."

"Okay, Ms. Webster." Before Marge could move, Luke was out of the car and came around to open the door for her. "Nice day for a walk," he said. "Summer's winding down. It'll be fall soon. "

"Yes." She smiled. "You can feel it in the air." It seemed, despite Piero Massione's childish behavior, the world was full of smiles now.

"You sure can. Need to enjoy what's left of the good weather." Luke smiled, too. "Have a good one," he said, and he got back into the car.

Marge watched the big black town car blend in with the rest of the traffic—the moving mass of other big black town cars and boxy yellow taxis, the private cars, the buses, and the trucks that made the city feel always on the go.

She turned away and smiled again; she'd just slipped out of the day's tightly packed schedule and found a little escape time just for herself. It didn't happen often. It certainly didn't happen often enough. She really needed just a small escape—needed to get away from her mental to-do list. She took one big, deep breath and looked around, looked to see where she had landed.

It was an ordinary neighborhood street, somewhere in the Village. Small shops, some brownstones, people just quietly going about their business. Babies in strollers. Dogs being walked. Teenagers falling in love. A city street. Always a treat. Better than any television screen for variety, humanity, action, the potential for drama, a laugh, something new.

She took off her jacket, hooked it over her arm and started to walk. A man passed her, turned to look, and kept going. At the corner, a street vendor was filling the air with the irresistible aroma of honey roasted nuts. She paused at his cart, checked her watch once more—forty minutes till she had to meet Bridey—decided she could indulge in a snack before lunch. She paid her dollar and started to walk away with her paper bag of honey roasted peanuts. But an idea stopped her. She turned and watched as a mother and her little boy approached the cart. The mother gave her boy the money to buy a bag. And Marge thought about it.

Street food in New York. Surprisingly, it really is very good. Good, and often very interesting. Might be an idea to discuss with Bridey. See what she thought of a piece on the street food of New York. It would make an amusing story. "What to Wear While Dining Out." With the emphasis on "out," of course.

Always new ideas. Can't help it. I just love the magazine so much.

She really needed to take more breaks like this one.

I know. I know. Doctor Diaz says I have to ease up a little. Working too hard.

She did a little deep breathing, quietly, as she walked along. Marge would never let anyone know, but it was beginning to worry her. Carrying it all on her shoulders. She was feeling the stress, she was seeing the signs of overwork, the wound-up overdrive of her thoughts that kept her from falling asleep. The little wrinkles forming at her lips. The need for concealer under her eyes.

But who would—who *could*—run *Lady Fair* as skillfully as she did? Marge knew it was her ability to be the calm in the eye of the storm that was her major asset—that had gotten her hired for this job at the impossibly early age of twenty-nine.

She'd first come to the notice of the magazine's owners early on, when she was a young features editor, first months on the job, and an article of hers won an ASME award. Not bad for a rookie. Not bad for *anyone*! Then, a month later, there was her memo to upper management suggesting a cost-cutting digital innovation that resulted in an annual bottom-line savings of more than eighty thousand dollars. And the clincher came the day a crazy ex-con broke through the lobby security downstairs and ran naked through *Lady Fair's* reception area, waving a long Tanaka knife. While the receptionist cringed behind her chrome and glass desk, paralyzed with terror, and the staff trembled in the corridors and behind their locked doors, it was the still-a-rookie Marge whose gentle and sympathetic voice talked the man down and kept him quiet until the police arrived to escort him out of the building, wrapped up in a gorgeous blue floral wool-and-silk shawl from Gucci, produced at the last minute by one of the design people, out of the nearest fashion closet.

When an ABC reporter did the interview about the incident for the evening news, Marge credited the outfit she'd been wearing. "It was probably the charcoal gray Valentino I had on. It's a very no-nonsense business suit, suitable for handling any office crisis. Maybe," she added, "he thought I was his parole officer."

But it wasn't only Marge's steel in the face of danger together with her light touch that got her noticed. She was a brilliant writer, knew how to work to a deadline, and understood the difference between a good story and an indispensable story. She'd proven she understood the dollars and cents of the industry, and she had a respect for its full product range from the low end of a strip mall's ready-to-wear to the *haute couture* of the most exclusive *salons*. And, perhaps the most important skill in a potential editor in chief, Marge had not only a passion for fashion but a sure sense of its exact place in today's social scene as well as in the scene that would appear over tomorrow's horizon.

What no one included in the mix, not even Marge herself, was what it was costing her to be cool and effective, day in and day out. No one, that is, except Dr. Martine Diaz who had been telling her to take it easier.

* * * *

She continued walking and nibbling on the nuts. Licking the honey off her fingertips. This little break in her day was precious. Nothing like a walk on a sweet day like this to put everything in its proper place.

She passed a small neighborhood park. To one side of the park, there was a playground. Children playing on swings and seesaws, with pull toys, and in a sandbox. Mothers on the benches, chatting, keeping an eye on their kids. To the right of the playground, a basketball court where some teenagers, all boys, were playing an energetic game. A few girls—girlfriends, perhaps?—were clustered around the edges, watching, commenting on the game, sharing their secrets, giggling now and then. School wouldn't start till after Labor Day and they all had a few days more to be free—to be able to play all day. Marge stopped to watch for a while, looking through the chain link fence that separated them from the street. She remembered how it was to be young. Remembered how it was to be Marge Webster at fifteen.

And knowing she sure didn't want to go back there again. Not ever!

More kids came down the street and went into the park. Two boys, three girls. The girls joined the girls already watching the game, sat down with them on the benches, joined in the chatter. Clearly they all knew each other, probably from school. The boys joined the ballplayers. Big greetings all around, high fives among the boys, playful make-believe punches in the gut, on the arm, and hair tousling. A couple of boys peeled off and walked over to sit with the girls. The ball was tossed to the newcomers and play started again.

Marge was struck by the difference—compared with the physical exuberance of the boys, the behavior of the girls seemed almost sedate.

She was still thinking about that as she continued on her walk. And it was still in her thoughts half an hour later as she arrived at the restaurant. For a change, her mind was not on the magazine. It was not on fashion. For a little while, she had managed to take it far from work.

* * * *

Bridey had already arrived, ordered wine for them both, and was nibbling on a breadstick when Marge walked into the garden restaurant. Bridey was a true carrot-top and her halo of brilliant red curls caught the sunlight that filtered through the overhanging greenery. Marge spotted her instantly and she waved off the hostess who approached her. "I see her," she said, and hurried over to the table

"You look terrific," Bridey said, looking up from the manuscript she was reading.

Marge acknowledged the compliment with a smile and a nod. "I'm feeling good. I just had a nice long walk."

"In those heels?"

The heels were at least three and a half inches, from Prada.

"I'm fine. I really needed the break." She draped her jacket over the back of the chair and got herself settled down. "Next issue, the big one for the year, closes in two weeks, and as usual, there are always disasters waiting to happen. Had another one drop in my lap just before I left this morning. We'll take care of it, but boy, did I need to calm down." The waiter was right there and poured wine into her glass. She nodded a "thank you" to him, and continued. "Sometimes I get so damned mad. But when I do, I need to sit on it. You get mad at people who work for you, you wind up creating enemies and political entanglements all around, and then the whole organization is in chaos." She could feel her stress level rising again and took a deep breath to calm down. "So it was really therapeutic to just stroll around before I came here. I feel much better now." She picked up the glass, swirled the wine a bit, and took a sip. "And there was something I saw while I was walking. Down near Bleecker Street, made me think.

I'd stopped to watch some kids in a playground playing basketball. And it's still on my mind."

She paused, trying to find the right words.

"Yes?"

"I was thinking. Bridey, do you ever want to be a little girl again?"

"Are you kidding? Why would I want to do that? I'm still trying to grow up." She laughed and set her manuscript to one side.

"That's what I was thinking. Maybe I'm wrong, but as I was walking here, I was thinking about all the women I know—have ever known. It must be hundreds, maybe thousands. And I can't think of a single woman I've ever known who wants to be a little girl again. Oh, every woman wants to *look* young, of course. But that's a different thing. I mean *be* a kid again. To act like a kid. Seems to me, no matter what her age, women seem to want to keep growing. Or, at least, seem to think they're somehow going to keep getting better. I don't know. It's a fuzzy idea."

"Do you think men are different?"

"Well, that's what I mean. I was watching these boys on the playground, in their basketball game. Being just—I don't know—just so young. And I've seen lots of grown men, much older men, when they get together— it's like they go back to being kids again. It's like no matter how old they get to be, they keep wanting to be little boys. They greet each other, play together, like kids. "

"I don't know—"

Marge seemed irritated with herself. "I'm not saying it well. I don't know what I mean, exactly. Like I said, it's a fuzzy notion. Maybe not all men, I suppose." The waiter arrived to take their order and she picked up the menu. "I'll have to think about it some more. Figure out what I mean." She glanced at the menu but didn't need it. She always ordered the same thing. She smiled at the waiter and said, "I'll have the grilled asparagus salad. But instead of the hollandaise, do you think—"

"I know, Ms. Webster." He interrupted her. "Just some lemon juice and pepper."

"You're a dear," she said. "And a cappuccino." She handed the menu to him. "That'll be all."

Bridey ordered a hamburger and sweet potato fries. And a small green salad. The waiter took her menu and disappeared.

The manuscript she'd been reading was on the table in front of her, and she opened her tote bag to put it away.

"Is that for the new book?" Marge asked. "Or your next column? For us?"

"It's the column. For the December issue."

"The 'Christmas in Scandinavia' theme. And you still proof on paper?"

"It's a good check. I miss a lot on screen."

"You're so old-fashioned."

"I know. Serves me well."

"Mack loves you that way."

"Mack is old-fashioned, too. In a way."

"Jerry is, too. Sort of."

"I know."

"We're both lucky."

"I guess."

They were both quiet for a moment.

Bridey spoke first. "So, what other deep thoughts have you been having on your way over here?"

"Actually, an idea for you." She took a breadstick from the basket. "You know those carts you see on the streets around town. The ones that sell roasted nuts. The honey-roasted kind?"

"I know. I could eat bags of the peanuts. Those are my favorite. And I love how the aroma fills up the whole street."

"Exactly. Well, I bought some while I was walking. And while I was eating them, I was thinking of all the great street food we have here in New York. Not just hot dogs. You can get Ethiopian and Chinese and Indonesian and Peruvian and God-knows-what-else. And it's all really good. So I was thinking about doing a 'Cart Food in New York' theme, with fashion to go with each one. Just a thought. But I think there's something there and I'm going to work on it. What do you think?"

"It would work."

"Maybe call it 'What to Wear While Dining Out.'"

Bridey smiled. "That's cute. I like it. And it would be fun research for me."

"I might join you. I could really use the break."

Bridey waited a minute—choosing her words. Then, gently, she said, "You work awfully hard, Marge." She looked seriously at her friend. "Is it okay to tell you?" She paused, then not waiting, she plunged on ahead. "You're looking—tired."

"Oh, Bridey. Not you, too." She took a sip of her wine. "My doctor's been telling me to take a rest."

"She's right."

"Okay, okay. You don't need to nag me." She took another breadstick and gestured with it as she talked. "Tell you what. As soon as this next issue is out, I'll take a vacation. Promise. Jerry's tied up in some big litigation for the foreseeable future so I'll hardly get to see him anyway."

"Promise?"

"Promise." The waiter was there with her asparagus and Bridey's burger, so she paused while he set it all down, offered the additional twists of pepper, made sure they had everything they wanted, then disappeared. She continued, "And here's a thought. How about let's do it together. You and me, without the guys, just a girls' week out of town. Or at least a few days. We could go to Cape Cod or even a Caribbean island, someplace gorgeous, and drink wine and loaf in the sun. What do you think?"

"I think you need a whole lot more than a week and I'd be lucky to be able to spare even that much."

"Oh, come on. Mack can take care of the kids for a few days. He'd love it. He's great with them and it wouldn't hurt you to take a short trip without them. It'll be an interesting change."

Bridey laughed. "Are you kidding? I know what you're doing, Marge. Like when we were kids. You'll wind up getting me into some kind of mischief."

"Who, me?" Marge laughed, too. "No way. I'm all grown up now. Those days are over. It's a rest I need, not excitement." She squeezed a bit of lemon on her salad. "Have dinner tonight with Jerry and me. We can talk about it some more. "

"Sounds nice. I'll check with Mack and get back to you."

"Great," Marge said. "Galba's at seven." And then, as though she'd flipped a switch, she slipped abruptly back into "professional" mode. "But this is a business lunch. We need to talk about your TV segment next week. So let's forget about vacations for now." She took a file of notes out of her bag and laid them next to her plate.

"Right," Bridey said. "Back to work." And there was no more talk of vacations.

Chapter Two

Piero Massione arrived all Italian charm and air-kisses, with his signature white hair flowing, and a pale leather jacket slung cape-like over his shoulders.

"Marge, *mia cara*, you look wonderful."

"And so do you, Piero. Young and handsome as ever. But you bring me disturbing news."

The tiny flicker of anxiety in Piero's eyes didn't match the broad, confident smile he was putting on, as though the two parts of his face were from two different people.

He didn't want to displease Marge Webster. No one wanted to displease Marge Webster. The photographers, the designers, the distributors—her approval was essential to everyone's success. Despite the surface cordiality, Piero was afraid of her. They were all afraid of her.

"Alas, Marge. What can I say? I am an artist. I cannot give you anything but my best work. And I was not happy with these latest."

"You know we close in two weeks."

What game is he playing? Does he think I'll let him re-negotiate his billings?

"Of course. But what can we do?"

Piero is a brilliant fashion photographer. But he shouldn't try to swim with the sharks—

"We can re-shoot, of course. If we need to. But you have access to the digital originals?"

"Of course."

"Have your people send them. Max will see what we can do." Maximilian Kovacs was *Lady Fair's* brilliant design editor and Marge trusted him to spin magic gold out of whatever Piero could provide, because whatever he'd shot, Marge knew they could work with it. There were a thousand ways to manipulate photographs to make them usable. "In the meantime, have a coffee and tell me about your flight." She signaled her assistant, Frieda, who had been alerted to be ready with an espresso. "You always meet such interesting people."

Piero pouted but he made his call to his studio in Milan. The pictures would be sent electronically. O brave new world! Then he took a seat and he and Marge chatted together, like old friends. Which, of course, they still were.

All would be well. Another disaster averted.

* * * *

Galba's Café was fizzy with the dinnertime buzz and clink of a popular Midtown restaurant. A couple of heads turned as the *maître d'* escorted Marge to the table, but most people were too cool to make a show of recognizing her. When Bridey came in, a few minutes later, a few more heads turned. People knew her delicious TV personality on the *Your Turn, Chef* cooking show and a discreet trail of smiles followed her as she threaded her way through the tables to join Marge.

"The guys aren't here yet?" as she sat down.

"No, we're ahead of them."

Bridey stowed her bag at her feet. "So," she said. "Did you get your latest disaster resolved?"

"Oh, sure. Just needed a little genius-massaging. It will work out. It always does."

"It does because you make it work out. But I know, Marge. It's a crisis-a-minute."

"That's just about it." Marge closed her eyes wearily, sighed briefly, then smiled. "But I do love my work."

"And you do a great job. *Lady Fair* is the best!"

"I know it is." She could say that to Bridey, without bragging, because they were old friends. "I know it is, Bridey."

"As long as you stay healthy."

Marge made a face and said, "Let's change the subject."

"I'm just saying. You look like you could use a little time in the sun. Maybe if you put on a little lipstick."

"Oh, jeez. I ran out so fast, I forgot."

"See? My point exactly. Since when do you forget to keep your face perfectly made up? That's really not like you."

"I know. I know." She was getting her little makeup kit out of her bag. "Some color will help."

Marge took a quick look at her face in the mirror, and frowned.

"Let's face it," Marge said. "I'm not twenty anymore."

She held the mirror up real close.

"That's for sure." Bridey was laughing. "Those days are long gone. And thank God for that. I wouldn't be twenty again for anything. I remember when you and I didn't have two pennies between us to rub together."

Marge touched a finger to the faint—very faint—beginning of a crease at the corner of her eye.

"I'm not thirty anymore, either."

"Just put on your lipstick, and stop feeling sorry for yourself. You look terrific and you know it."

"In a few years I'll be forty."

"You're thirty-five and much too young to be mourning your lost youth."

"I know. I know. I'm just tired." Marge brushed a bit of color onto her lips. "Working too hard, too much to think about." A last glance into the mirror and she stowed it and the lipstick into her makeup case, zipped it up, and dropped the case into her handbag. "I need a rest. That's all there is to it."

"Maybe when the September issue closes?"

"I'll think about it, Bridey. I really will." Marge brushed a tiny wisp of lint from her jacket, sat back in her chair and put a smile on her face. "The guys will be here in a minute and I just want a cheery dinner with my best friends."

"That's better," Bridey said. She broke off a bit of bread from the basket and dipped it into the tiny dish of olive oil the waiter had set between them. "Honestly, Marge. Have you any idea how many women would die for the life you have? You're healthy, you're beautiful, you have the greatest job in the world. Designers plead with you to wear their clothes, they give you enough gorgeous stuff to outfit the whole Upper East Side, plus accessories, and buckets of makeup no ordinary human being can afford. How much does that lipstick cost?"

"It's ninety dollars retail. Louboutin's latest."

"I didn't know it was possible to spend ninety dollars on a lipstick. And the suit?"

"You don't want to know. It would make you mad."

"Thank you for that." Bridey's face reflected the sarcasm. "You live in a gorgeous apartment that cost millions, and you have a great, successful, good-looking guy in love with you, who'd move in with you in a minute if you'd let him. And I know he's proposed, at least twice. Mack told me. Jerry Germaine thinks you're absolutely the best thing that ever happened in his whole life—"

"I know."

"—and who really is maybe the best thing that ever happened in *your* life."

"Well—maybe—"

"Marge, you know I'm right."

"I know."

"So that's enough, Ms. Webster. We're both totally lucky and I don't want to hear another word."

"You're right. Of course."

"Now drink your wine and stop looking so snarky."

* * * *

When Jerry arrived, ten minutes later, it was with a smile, a quick kiss for Marge, and a single red rose, which he presented to her with a small flourish. "Guy outside was selling these and I couldn't resist," he said. "It's my apology for being late." He looked at the empty fourth chair. "Where's Mack? Is he late, too?"

"He texted," Bridey said. "Got hung up in traffic. He'll be here soon. Said to go ahead and order without him."

"Great," he said. "I'm starving. No time for lunch—just a bag of pretzels and a Coke out of a vending machine."

"How's the trial going?" Marge was putting the rose into her water glass. "You finished jury selection?"

"Yeah. Too early to tell, but all good so far. Guy on the other side will be tough."

"You'll win," she said. "You always do."

How could he not give her a big smile? He did, a smile that took in Bridey as well, and maybe the whole restaurant. And he leaned over to Marge and kissed her again. "You are my best cheering squad. Couldn't do it without you, honey."

"It's mutual, Jerry." Marge returned the kiss. "And you're *my* cheering squad."

"Okay, okay, you two," Bridey said. "Enough of that. I'm starving, too. Let's order."

"Right," Jerry said, and signaled the waiter who came right over, order pad in hand. In a few minutes, a nice Italian red wine was being poured, they were sharing a plate of antipasti for the table, and were talking about vacation possibilities.

"I'm all for it," Jerry was saying, "And I think we should make plans. But this trial's going be a long one so there's no way I can commit to anything for at least a month—could be more. Maybe you two could take off a little time together. See if Mack could join you."

"I know he can't," Bridey said. "He needs to be in New York for the Expo thing this month. But Marge and I were talking about it. I think Mack would be able to handle the kids for a few days anyway to let me get away for a quick vacation. I've really been pushing Marge to get a rest—"

She broke off, because Mack had just arrived and she waved to him as she saw him looking around for them. "Speak of the devil," she said.

And there was Mack, also bearing a single red rose.

"Hi, everyone," he said. "Sorry I'm late." He handed the rose to Bridey and said, "There's a guy outside selling these." He kissed her and said, "For you, honey. Traffic was all snarled coming down Lexington." He pulled out the empty chair and got himself settled. He saw the rose in Marge's water glass and he laughed.

"Hey, Jerry, so you were late, too?"

"I got hung up at court. Couldn't get away earlier."

"Big case?"

"Big enough. The girls were talking about taking a vacation, but I'll be tied up with this thing for weeks. I can't get away now, not for a couple of months, at least." He turned to Marge and said, "But honey, maybe I can make it up a bit. The client gave me a couple of tickets to the game tomorrow night. Courtside. At the Garden. Want to go?"

"Are you kidding? Of course I want to go."

"My time might be a little tight tomorrow, so why don't you meet me at the courthouse so we can grab a cab and go together."

She nodded, big smile, and it was arranged.

Mack said, "Hey Jerry—how about those Knicks? You think they'll make it this year?"

Jerry was instantly animated—all thoughts of jury selection, strategy to brainstorm, millions of bucks at risk—all slipped away and the men were boys again.

Marge tipped her head at Bridey and her little smile spoke for her.

See what I mean? Look at them. No matter how grown-up they are, they connect so easily with each other in their world of play. Like little boys

They reminded her of the pick-up game she'd watched earlier that day, the male of the species, bonding in its love of sports, a love rooted in their little-boy lives, never outgrown. And why should it be? No matter how solemn their work may be, they could always tap back into their little-boyness.

She observed the two men with admiration. With wonder. And with pleasure. She was comparing the two men.

Look at them. Bridey's a lucky woman. They are such an attractive couple.

Bridey Berrigan, with her delicate features, her creamy complexion, framed by the brilliant red curls—Marge had always imagined her friend as the daughter of an Irish fairy mother and a leprechaun father—a mischievous child, grown now into a reliable, busy and productive professional. She was still trim, not a single extra pound had been added to her fine, slim frame since having her two absolutely darling children, five-year-old Llewellyn, named for his grandfather, and Henrietta, about to have her second birthday in a few weeks.

Bridey made a lovely counterpart to Mack whose dark hair and almost black eyes contrasted so attractively with her colorful beauty. Mack was an ex-Navy man, and he had the good looks of a fit, healthy, well-bred, conservative executive. Book publisher, actually. From the neat trim of his haircut down to the mirror-shine of his black shoes, Mack Brewster was every inch, outwardly, the conservative, by-the-book man he'd been brought up to be. But Bridey had brought merriment and magic into his well-managed life and he adored her. Marge thought they were a physically beautiful and emotionally perfectly matched couple.

Her own Jerry—she always thought of him as "her" Jerry—was a different type altogether. Good-looking, too, but in a different way. He had a bit of the absent-minded professor about him. A killer in the courtroom, but never could find his keys, his wallet, the book he'd been reading. She wondered if she and Jerry—like Bridey and Mack—were a "good-looking couple."

She thought it was sweet of Bridey to have said she was beautiful, but Marge was around professionally gorgeous women all day every day, and she knew what great beauty looked like. She didn't think of herself as beautiful. Okay-looking, she thought, but not beautiful. Her features were regular, the teeniest bump at the bridge of her nose, very deep-blue eyes (she really liked her eyes which were slightly almond-shaped), her hair was dark, thick and a little hard to keep under control. But what woman likes her own hair? She didn't worry much about it. It was professionally styled—it had to be because of the position she held—and right now she'd have been wearing it dressed low to the nape of her neck, but just before she left the office to come to the restaurant, she'd pulled the pins out, shook her hair loose, and let it fall naturally just past her shoulders.

She supposed she and Jerry looked good together. Was that important? They got along well, but she never felt as though they needed to live together in order to get along well. They were sort of bonded. Casually bonded. Was that enough?

The waiter arrived with their food, and for a moment there was a flurry of arranging plates and tasting the first bites and making observations about the skill of the chef. They were old friends and had long ago gotten into the rather intimate habit of tasting each other's food. Soon the four of them were in a heated political discussion, the kind that can animate good friends without sending them home mad. By the time they'd had their desserts, paid the bill, and were ready to leave, they'd set aside all their political differences, which weren't many and in any case, not crucial, and were ready to end the day.

Out on the street, Mack and Bridey said good night and were walking home in the sweet late-summer evening. Jerry scanned the street for a cruising cab and it was only a minute before a yellow taxi pulled up. He held the door and Marge got in.

He leaned his head into the cab.

"Don't forget. Tomorrow night. Meet me at the courthouse. Six o'clock."

"I didn't forget."

"Great. We'll ride uptown together—grab dinner somewhere before the game. See you then."

He closed the door, and the taxi drove off.

She sat back, leaned her head against the cracking faux leather, smiled, and started planning.

Courtside at the Garden. Cameras likely, of course. Wear something casual, something simple. Altuzarra sent over some great skirts this afternoon. Maybe one of those—the multicolored maxi skirt, I think. With tall boots. And a plain top, something loose and comfy. And long sleeves. They keep the Garden so cold.

And after the game—Jerry will come back to the apartment with me. Maybe he'll stay for the weekend.

A nice thought. She liked having Jerry Germaine in her life.

The city flowed past her, bright lights flashing in the dark, the reds and the greens of the traffic signals, and the New York pulse all around her. She put her head back, closed her eyes, and smiled all the way home.

Chapter Three

Friday afternoon, already six o'clock, and Marge hurried down the corridor just as the doors to the courtroom were being opened. There was a spill of people coming out, but she knew Jerry wouldn't be among those first to leave. He'd need to be packing up his papers, having some last words with his team, with his client, maybe even in the judge's chambers along with opposing counsel, needing to take care of some loose ends. So she got herself comfortable on a bench opposite the doors, took out her tablet and prepared to get a little work handled while she waited. A young new features editor, Penny Lightly, had just joined the staff and had pitched a proposal, the first one on her own. Marge started scrolling through it and was pleased, right away. The girl was onto a good idea, something that would appeal to a certain niche of *Lady Fair* readers, and she had a nice writing style, conversational but sophisticated. Though the hall was filled with the chatter of people and the sounds of their footsteps on the marble floor, Marge was quickly engrossed, unbothered by the clatter around her. Unbothered, unaware.

Until a man's voice broke through the background noise.

"My God! Marge? Marge Webster? Is that you?"

That voice.

Her hand went to her throat.

The necklace!

So many years ago, she still knew that voice.

She looked up. He was silhouetted against the ceiling light behind him; his face was shadowed. A sheaf of papers in one hand, cell phone in the other, business suit, and his tie slightly askew. But yes, of course she remembered him.

"Sam?"

Back in high school, he'd been a tall, skinny boy, not athletic, wrote for the school newspaper and the literary magazine. Funny, fun, bright, charismatic and everyone loved him. Went on to Harvard undergrad. Her family moved out of state. They'd gone on to separate lives, lost track of each other.

"What in the world—?"

He stuck the cell phone in his pocket. Laid the papers on the bench and sat down next to her.

"I know," he said. "What in the world? What are you doing here?"

"I'm waiting to meet—someone." She'd been about to say "my boyfriend," and noticed that she'd edited herself.

"You're looking great," Sam said. He seemed really happy to see her. "I see you sometimes, in the news. I tell people, 'I knew her, back in high school.'" He laughed. "They always want to know, 'What's she really like?'"

"What do you tell them?" She couldn't believe how she felt—totally self-conscious—like she was a teenager again. She'd gone tongue-tied and could feel herself blushing.

"I tell them you were the most focused kid I'd ever known, that you knew what you were going to be doing in ten years, in twenty years. And that you were always got up in the most interesting, God-awful outfits. Something new and outrageous every day. Plus, that you were a knockout. The best-looking girl in the school." He paused and his face lost some of its merriment. "And that you left a trail of broken hearts behind you."

She managed a little laugh and found her tongue. "I don't know whether to protest or say thank you. I wasn't aware of any broken hearts."

He laughed, too. Reassuringly. "We were all young. I'm sure we all recovered."

"Well, then. No damage done."

"No, none at all." There was that nice smile of his. "Listen. We ought to go somewhere and catch up. Are you busy? There's a bar, right across Centre Street, we could—"

"Can't do it, Sam. I'm busy tonight." She noticed that she didn't say "I have a date." Second time she'd edited herself. "Going to the game at the Garden." She felt as though she needed to change the subject. "Have you kept in touch with people from school?"

"Some of them." He paused, noticed the shift. "But listen. Let's really plan to get together. I could give you a call—arrange something—"

"Of course," Marge said. *I can't believe this. My hand is shaking.* She needed to get her hand under control. She dug around in her bag, fished out her business card, and handed it to him. "Call me. Any time. We can dredge up old memories. If I can remember back that far."

They were laughing together when Jerry came out of the courtroom.

"Oh, here he is, now," she said. Jerry spotted them together as she lifted a hand to wave him over. His expression, as he approached them, seemed guarded, even—perhaps—not his usually cordial smile? *That's not like Jerry,* she thought. *What's bothering him?*

"Jerry," she said, "this is Sam Packard. He just found me here while I was waiting for you. Sam and I were in high school together. Big surprise, running into each other like this—after all these years." And to Sam, she said, "Sam, this is Jerry Germaine. I've been waiting for him to finish up. We're going to the game tonight." To her surprise, the two men didn't shake hands. She paused, wondering what was going on. "I was going to suggest Sam join us for dinner. He could tell you all about my awkward adolescent years. Sam was three years ahead of me in school and we all adored him. He was—"

But Sam interrupted her. He turned to Jerry and shrugged and said, "If I'd known—"

Jerry's smile was a forced imitation of the real thing.

"Sam and I know each other, honey. Sam's on the other side." His tone was cool, only professionally cordial. Cautious—and maybe just a little sarcastic? "My 'worthy opponent.'"

"I had no idea, Jerry," Sam said. "Marge didn't say—"

"Of course not." Jerry's tone was just this side of frosty.

Sam got the message. He smiled—and Marge remembered that smile of his, remembered how it slipped across his face and lit up his nice brown eyes, a merry little smile that acknowledged that life always takes such an amusing turn.

He picked up the sheaf of papers from the bench. "Let's put a hold on that dinner," he said. "Maybe when this case is done, we could all get together and talk about the good old days." To Jerry, he said, "We can talk about how Marge and I were once young and innocent." And to Marge he said, "I've got to get back to the office. It was great running into you like this. Really, Marge." Now the two men did shake hands. And Sam said, "See you back here on Monday, Jerry." And he was gone.

Marge put away her tablet. Silently, she and Jerry walked down the corridor to the courthouse doors and out into the late afternoon light, down the long, broad flight of stone steps out to Centre Street. They remained silent until they were in the cab headed uptown. Then Jerry spoke.

"So. Imagine your knowing Sam Packard."

"Mm-hmm. Yeah."

They continued on silently for a while.

Then Marge said, "I think I'd heard he went to law school. It was a long time ago."

"Well, when this case is over, I suppose we could all go have a drink together or something. You could catch up."

"Yeah. We could do that."

She was deep in her memories and didn't see how Jerry was looking at her. Very thoughtfully.

Chapter Four

"It was like a thunderbolt," Marge said. "I swear, Bridey. Like I'd been hit by lightning."

Marge and Bridey were at their favorite brunch place, Miss Muffett's Tea Shop on Madison Avenue. Miss Muffett's people served the loveliest little sandwiches and tea cakes, had perhaps a hundred teas available, and were serious about their organic menu. Marge and Bridey had each ordered omelets and toast, and the waitress had set their plates in front of them and gone to get their tea—an exotic infused floral for Bridey, plain Earl Grey for Marge.

"You've got to swear to say nothing to anyone, Bridey. Not even Mack." She looked miserable.

"Of course not. Just tell me what happened."

"I don't know what to say, Bridey. There he was, big as life, right there in the courthouse, and I was like I was fourteen years old again, like my head was full of oatmeal and I couldn't think what to say. Like I was a dumb kid again."

"I can believe it. You just said 'like' three times."

Marge shrugged. "Like I said. A dumb kid again."

"You were never a dumb kid, Marge. Not even in high school."

"Okay. Maybe not—but I was sure dumb about Sam Packard." She broke off a bit of toast and buttered it. "You remember?"

"I remember. He was a senior and you were totally goofy about him. For months, totally goofy. I remember, you had a party for your fifteenth birthday and he came and he gave you a little necklace. It was a silver chain with some kind of charm. You wore that damn necklace all the time. Whatever happened to it?"

Marge shrugged. "Oh, I don't know. I've forgotten." That was a lie. Marge knew perfectly well where that necklace was—in a small jewelry bag, a pouch made of royal purple velvet—tucked safely away in a corner of her jewel box. "It was so long ago," she said.

"He took you to his senior prom. You were just a freshman and he took you to his senior prom."

"Yes, he did. It was a big deal."

"It was a *really* big deal. We were all in awe."

"I was in awe myself." Marge laughed at the memory.

"What was it about Sam Packard? It's not like he was the hottest-looking guy in the school. But he was so popular. He was everyone's best friend."

"I know. I remember—he was funny—not funny-looking. Just funny. He made me laugh."

"He made everyone laugh. Is he still skinny and sort of gangly? Is his hair still all kind of wild?"

"No. It looked quite normal. Still that sort of dark sandy color. Quite tidy, in fact. Actually, he's aged nicely. He's kind of filled out, looks more mature now." She laughed. "Well, of course, what am I saying? He *is* more mature. He must be close to forty."

"Is he married?"

"I didn't have a chance to ask. He didn't say."

"No ring?"

"I had no chance to look. Actually, I didn't think of it."

"I remember his eyes," Bridey said. "He had the nicest eyes."

"I guess that was it. I was looking at his eyes. Didn't think to look at his hand."

"So what did you talk about?"

"We didn't have a chance, really, to talk about anything. He suggested we get together, have a drink or something, catch up on old times, and I swear, Bridey, my heart just went pit-a-pat, it really did, like I couldn't breathe. But just then Jerry came out of the courtroom before I could even answer."

"Are you going to see him?"

Marge didn't answer right away. Then, almost to herself, she said, "I really want to. I really would. Oh, Bridey, I really do want to." She looked at the toast in her hand and took a bite. She hadn't touched her omelet at all. "But I shouldn't. I shouldn't even be feeling this way about him." She looked at the eggs on her plate as though she wondered how they got there. She had absolutely no appetite at all. She pushed the plate away. "Anyway, I really can't. At least, not while they have this case against each other. It would be sort of unethical—or, at least—I don't know—it wouldn't look right. When a lawyer's in court every day, litigating something, his girlfriend shouldn't be seen socializing with the lawyer on the other side. Doesn't look right."

"But you do want to see him?"

"I really do. Is that awful of me?"

"I'm not sure. When you called this morning, you said you hardly slept last night. Is it that bad?"

"Like I said, it was like a lightning bolt. No kidding. There he was and suddenly I was back in that time when I had been so in love—the way you can be in love only when you're fourteen—like I thought magic flowed from his fingertips."

"Oh, Marge, I don't know whether to laugh or cry. You can't be serious."

"I know. I can't be. Bridey, I'm thirty-five years old. I'm a serious adult. I live a very serious, adult life. I manage a major corporate enterprise, I influence a billion-dollar industry. Grown-up people invest big money depending on what I say, the choices I make. And a boy from my youth shows up and I'm fourteen years old again. I feel like a fool." She looked at the toast in her hand, decided she didn't want it, put it back on the plate. Fourteen silly years old again," she repeated. "And it was as though the years fell off me and I was dumb again in that sweet way it is when you're too young to know how dumb you are. Do you understand? Do you remember?"

"Hmm." Bridey smiled. "What I remember is I don't ever want to be that dumb again."

"Well, that's just it. What I'd forgotten is how *sweet* it is. Oh, God, Bridey. It's like I have to save me from myself. What am I going to do?"

"Where's Jerry today?"

"He's at the club. Playing tennis. And that's another thing. I think maybe Jerry smelled a rat. You know what a good guy Jerry is, how easy-going. But right away they were like a couple of moose or rams or something, squaring off against each other. I felt the tension between them, the minute Jerry saw me with him."

"That's only because they're on opposite sides in the case. They have to be adversaries. In court at least. Until it's over."

"I guess so. You mean it's not me?" She was definitely uncertain. "Probably. I suppose you're right."

"Of course I'm right." She signaled the waitress for more tea. "Now eat your omelet and stop being fourteen again. Go home and get on your treadmill. Work up a sweat. It will clear your head."

"I already did that. At five o'clock this morning. It didn't help."

"Jerry must have loved that. Didn't your pounding away on the treadmill wake him up?"

"He said he didn't mind. He's an early riser anyway and he said he could use the time to work on a brief before he went to play tennis. I told him I had a busy schedule today and wanted to get an early start."

Bridey made some playful *tsk-tsking* sounds. "Lying to your boyfriend. Shame on you, Marge. That's not good." Her smile said she wasn't really scolding.

But still, Marge felt guilty.

"Not really lying," she said, trying to reassure herself. "Just keeping the peace."

"Just kidding, Marge. But I know you, and Jerry does, too. You'd never be up at five. Work days, yes, but never on a Saturday."

"No. Actually, I really do have to get to the office today." At least that part was true.

But the rest of it she wasn't ready to share with Bridey. Not yet. She wasn't ready to tell Bridey that at five that morning, when she gave up trying to sleep, she found a text message on her phone.

A message from Sam.

So good to run into you, Marge.

Beautiful as always—beautiful as I remembered you. When we're done with this case, I want to see you.

Chapter Five

She wasn't lying when she said she needed to be in the office that day. An item in the late news last night had caught her attention.

And anything that took her mind off Sam Packard was a welcome distraction.

It was something in the business report. Something about Crackerbox Publications. Something she thought would tie in well with Penny Lightly's pitch.

So she'd left an early-morning text for Penny to meet her at the office at noon. And now, after she left Miss Muffet's Tea Shop, while Luke drove her downtown, she had a chance to follow up on the story from the morning newspaper's business section.

Penny was already at the office when Marge arrived.

"Maybe you've heard of Crackerbox?"

"Don't they publish those Benny Bunny books for little kids? Where Benny is a detective who solves mysteries at his day care?"

"That's the one. That, and the 'Wizard Works' series—science stories for young children. And lots more."

Penny nodded. "I've seen them. They're a major publisher of children's picture books, aren't they?"

"Right. And they've just announced they're acquiring a company that manufactures book-themed products for children. Characters from kids' books on tee shirts, kids' costumes and party supplies, mugs, novelty pencils. That sort of thing. I took the article from this morning's *Times*." She took the clipping out of her bag and handed it to Penny.

She waited a couple of minutes while Penny read quickly through the article.

Then she went on.

"The roll-out of the new products will be a week from this Friday. Right after our big issue hits the newsstands. We'll all be in recovery mode then, and I'll be in the mood for a party. You will be, too."

Penny nodded.

"The Crackerbox launch will be at The Spire. That's a new event spot in Brooklyn, at the top of that fancy new commercial skyscraper in the downtown business section. Just opened a couple of months ago."

"I don't live very far from there and I watched the building go up. I was hoping I'd get to go up there some time, see the city from way up high."

"Here's your chance. We're going to go together. Crackerbox may not have thought to include a fashion magazine on their guest list, but I'm sure I can get us a couple of invitations. I'll make some phone calls. I liked the proposal you sent me, and I see a possible children's fashion piece here that would tie in nicely with it."

It was a pleasure to see Penny's face as she reacted to Marge's approval. All she said was, "Thank you, Marge." She was excited not only to have had the first pitch she'd made on her own get approved by Marge, but to have it be followed up immediately by its expansion into something bigger was a great confidence builder for the rookie editor.

She was eager to get started. Marge sat down with her, they went over what they knew about Crackerbox and its planned acquisition and product expectations. They strategized the form Penny's piece would follow. They talked over the length of the piece, the angle it would take, and a schedule for getting it into print. Marge got a kick out of watching the girl tackle her new assignment.

Her name suits her, she thought. *A bright penny. And she writes with a light touch. A nice combination.*

Marge hoped the rigors of the work and the years ahead of her wouldn't take off any of that shine. She wished her well, and Penny went off to get started.

Marge spent the next three hours catching up on marketing figures, ad revenues, other business matters. There was so much to keep up with. So much advertising was moving over to digital platforms, and Marge had decided to have *Lady Fair* take the lead in joining up with some of the fashion brands, taking the initiative to help them create digital advertising campaigns. In addition, the industry was beginning to reach its market through social media, creating an entirely new area of competition for *Lady Fair*—and for Marge—to deal with. The magazine's digital department had been growing at a remarkable rate and it was becoming clear they were going to need to hire more people and to expand their physical space some more.

It was almost five o'clock before Marge realized she was exhausted. Realized she hadn't eaten since her early breakfast with Bridey. Realized, too, that she hadn't slept last night. A headache had crept up on her, her eyes felt sandpapered, and she noticed a kind of odd thumping in her chest that was a brand new sensation. Also, an alarming tremor in her thumbs.

She dialed Jerry's cell phone.

"Where are you?" she asked, when he answered.

"Here. At your place. Working on a brief. And waiting for you. Where are you?"

"At the office. And I'm dog tired. I think I need some pampering."

"That's what I'm here for, honey. Don't do anything else tonight. Come home. I'll cook something and get you to bed early."

"You're such a good guy, Jerry."

"You work too hard, Marge."

"Probably. But there's so much to be done."

"I know."

* * * *

Jerry had thawed out a couple of steaks and had them peppered and ready to grill. By the time Marge arrived home, a big bowl of salad and a bottle of red wine were already on the table. He thought of lighting candles, too, but had decided that was pretentious. Good food and rest were what Marge needed, not romance. And indeed, that was exactly what Marge did need and want, a quiet, restful evening, curled up on the sofa with Jerry and maybe a little TV, a bowl of ice cream, and early to bed. She really was exhausted.

* * * *

She slept till nine thirty and when she woke up, Jerry was already on the sofa in the living room, working on his laptop. There were note pages all around him and he was looking intense. His hair was mussed—obviously not yet brushed—and he was still in his pajama bottoms. No top.

In the kitchen, she poured a cup of coffee and took a doughnut out of the bread box. The morning paper was on the counter and she glanced briefly at the front-page headlines while she ate the doughnut. Then she carried coffee and paper into the living room and sat down next to Jerry on the sofa.

"Okay to bother you?"

"Oh, God, yes! I need a break." He leaned back and ran his hands through his hair, as though that would help organize his thoughts.

"Thanks for letting me sleep."

"Feeling better?"

"Much."

He put an arm around her, pulled her close and kissed her cheek.

"You were talking in your sleep."

She didn't say anything for a moment. Then, "I sort of remember. What was I saying?"

Jerry laughed. "You were giggling. Something about a necklace. You kept saying, 'Put it away! Put it away!' And 'Look. It's a horse.' Didn't make any sense to me."

Now she remembered her dream, and she turned her face away from him. She picked up some of his notes and pretended to find them interesting. "Dreams never make any sense," she said. "Tell me about this case."

"You don't want to know."

"It's that bad?"

"Yeah. One of those international things—a British and Swiss investment outfit along with some Middle East money, they're buying a big stake in an oil company in Kazakhstan. Using a US partnership with an off-shore component, giving the Kazakhs a chance to pick up a chunk of cash—a few billion –with a fifteen-year buyback provision. The buyback is a cover-up. The Kazakhs need cash and this whole transaction is really a loan to them. All sorts of geo-political and anti-trust issues. The regulators are all over it."

"I'm already bored."

"I warned you."

"Is the deal legal?"

"Sure. At least, probably. But it's politically complicated, so all the parties want to keep it low key."

"Which one of these players is your client?"

"Our firm is representing the Swiss. And your friend, Sam Packard, he's with the regulators. The stock market will pay attention. No one else."

"Why don't you have one of your associates do the brief? Today is Sunday. You ought to take the day off."

"It's just a narrow legal point the judge asked for and I already have all the information. I can get it together quickly."

"You work too hard," she said.

He laughed. "Look who's talking. You're the one who works too hard. Makes you talk in your sleep. A sure sign of stress."

"Oh, I don't think so. You said I was giggling."

"No, it's true, Marge. You have been working too hard. I see the signs. You're not eating right, you've lost some weight. You're not sleeping well. And last night wasn't the first time. When this case is over, we should try to get away for a while."

"When will that be?"

"I don't know. Could be we wind it up quickly. Or it could take a couple of months, maybe more. But think about it. About getting away for a while. Maybe by then it will be January, February. We could do some skiing in Utah. Go to Park City for the Sundance Festival. Or something. Maybe the Caribbean, go somewhere warm and sunny. Let's think about it."

She snuggled up against him.

"Okay, Jerry. I'll think about it. I will. Really."

Chapter Six

But getting away would not be easy. At least, not for a while. Marge could leave her desk and she could walk out of her office, but she couldn't get away from her job. Fashion Week in Milan was about to take her to Italy for four days, followed immediately by the shows in Paris, days that were a dawn-to-midnight frenzy of activity. On her return, there were people to hire, others to fire, production problems, legal matters to review—a nasty copyright fight with one of her favorite authors, and a contract dispute with the company that ran the employees' cafeteria. There were interviews to give, TV appearances to fulfill, red carpet events, and social engagements, some obligatory and some too irresistibly fun to "regret." Everyone wanted her attention. And her time. And all of it had to be squeezed into these last days before the big issue closed.

Emotions always flared at this time of the year; the big annual issue exhausted everyone and the nervous breakdowns they promised themselves "when this is all over" would typically begin to erupt ahead of the scheduled publication date. Temper tantrums could be heard down the hallways and discreet sobbing behind closed office doors. Good friends lost all patience with each other and became "sworn enemies," at least until the kiss-and-make-up phase that inevitably followed these storm sessions. It was Marge's job to keep things running smoothly even as irritability meters dialed up higher and higher, and the entire staff relied on her to keep everyone from killing everyone. The staff relied on her because her hand on the tiller was famously steady and reassuring; Marge Webster had never been known to lose her temper and she always brought everyone through their emotional eruptions with a light touch and a gentle-but-firm solution that allowed them to remember that they really were grown-ups and a sense of perspective would get them past the immediate chaos. She had an eagle-eye for trouble and words of wisdom for everyone. She was a four-star general and a tender mama all in one good-looking package. She was talented, smart, and sane.

In other words, Marge was perfect.

Only, of course, she wasn't. Only the angels are perfect, and Marge was no angel. She had her blind spots. And the blindest one of all was her inability to dial her energy down and take a rest. So once again, she'd brought the big issue to fruition, and she was showered with praise, and she was told again how no one else could have done it so successfully, and they all went out to celebrate. She enjoyed her work so thoroughly, was so passionate about what she could do with *Lady Fair,* she didn't even realize she'd been working eighteen hours a day, going at maximum effort for weeks, definitely not eating right, and lately had been living on the canapés and crudités that were the fare at many of the events at which her presence was necessary. She was always too busy at these events, making useful professional connections and keeping up the obligatory small talk, to notice that she was practically starving herself.

* * * *

It was at the Crackerbox launch that the wake-up call finally arrived.

The event venue was a penthouse with wrap-around glass and heart-stopping views of rivers and bridges and miles of Brooklyn's new growth superimposed on its historic neighborhoods. Way down below, tiny vehicles and even tinier human beings were almost invisible, and in the distance, across the river, the skyscrapers of Manhattan's financial district rose imperiously, topped by the brand new Freedom Tower taking its place only a block beyond the old Woolworth Building, once—a hundred years ago—the tallest building in the world, the two structures together a measure of New York's growth as a financial and industrial giant.

Noisy chatter and music and the clink of glasses and the trill of laugher filled the space. Samples of Crackerbox's new products were displayed everywhere, and near the entrance, a table with goody bags filled with swag—novelty items, tee shirts, cards and coupons and fliers and pamphlets, all advertising the new venture. Crackerbox's officers and reps, the invited guests, and the uniformed catering staff were jammed into a swirling mass, and it was into this giddy, boozy, energetic crowd that Marge and Penny arrived. Marge had come along because she wanted to observe the young writer and see how she handled herself in this setting, but she'd been going since early that morning, had already fielded a half a dozen "crises," panic attacks, and other disasters, and had not had a chance to eat since the bagel she'd nibbled on while Luke drove her to the office ten hours earlier. She'd had a bad night—another one—imagining Jerry and Sam demanding her attention while squaring off against each other, along with the fantasy of herself being called into some celestial principal's office and being made to account for her wicked dreams. She was an exhausted set of nerve endings, and hadn't yet realized, she was on the verge of a collapse.

From a tray of wineglasses that passed by her, a small, round, silver tray carried by a cute young man—surely an out-of-work actor picking up a few bucks between auditions—she plucked a glass. She did a quick survey across the mob of heads, saw that the nearest bit of food was on a platter of something shrimp-y looking being carried by another young man across the room, and planned to spear a couple when it swam closer to her. She also saw Penny, nearby, in wide-eyed conversation with an older man Marge recognized as a member of Crackerbox's board of directors. Marge smiled to herself. *Good girl, Penny,* she said to herself. *I like the girl's style.*

And it was right at that moment that everything, shrimp and wine and talking heads and river views and ambient music all swirled together into a molten mass, like a four-year-old's finger paint masterpiece. She felt the blood in her feet turn hot and begin to boil up through her body. She knew she was about to faint, and a blur of panic filled her head. *Oh, God! Not a scene. Not here!* She dropped down onto a low hassock-like seat that—mercifully!—was right behind her.

To her amazement, Penny materialized out of nowhere and was kneeling right next to her.

Penny's whisper was urgent.

"What can I do?"

"Get me out of here," Marge whispered back.

With a single unobtrusive gesture, Penny took the wineglass from Marge's fingers, set it on a nearby table and had Marge up on her feet, her arm under Marge's arm. As she steered her toward the elevator, she snagged a passing waiter with her free hand, and with a decisive nod toward Marge, said a single word to him, under her breath.

"Water!"

Sharp young man, and he was off like a shot to the bar and back with a glass of water before the elevator arrived.

"Drink this," Penny said as the doors closed behind them. In the lobby she got Marge into one of the lounge chairs, took the glass from her fingers and put it on the floor next to the chair. "Get your head down, between your knees." Marge obeyed and hung her head way down, till her blood was back where it should be and the danger of fainting had passed.

Penny was leaning over her.

"Jeez, Marge. You okay? You scared the hell out of me."

Marge took a couple of deep breaths. She mentally checked her faculties, her heartbeat was calming down, and the fizziness in her head was subsiding. She wiggled her fingers and they seemed to be okay.

"I guess. Lucky for me you were there. Quick thinking, Penny. I owe you a big thank you."

"I just saw you go all pale and weak-kneed."

"I'm okay now. Embarrassed. But okay." She gave Penny a little smile. Penny smiled, too. "Have you had anything to eat today?"

"I guess not. Some days just get so busy. And I forget to eat."

"Why don't you sit here for a bit? I'll run outside and get you something."

"No, I'll be okay. My driver's here." She stood up—and immediately things began to swim again and she dropped back onto the chair.

"Whoops. Maybe not," she said.

"You stay here. I'll find a diner or deli or something. Be back in a sec."

Marge didn't protest anymore and Penny was gone through the revolving doors.

Marge got out her phone and dialed her doctor's office.

Thank God for concierge service. I've been putting this off too long.

In minutes, she had an appointment to see Dr. Diaz, first thing in the morning. Then she closed her eyes, put her head back, and rested until Penny was back, only ten minutes later, with a bottle of juice and a couple of protein power bars.

"You did good," she said to Penny, letting herself be ungrammatical.

Penny smiled. "Thank the Girl Scouts. Got my first-aid badge when I was fourteen." She opened one of the bars, handed it to Marge. "Here. You'd better get this down," and uncapped the bottle of juice. "And this, too." And after Marge had eaten and drunk, Penny said, "You okay now? Ready to get to your car? Do you think you ought to get to the ER?"

"Oh, no. That won't be necessary. I called my doctor and I'll see her in the morning. I'll be okay. Just need a good night's sleep." She stood up, a little tentatively, decided she was steady enough. "You've been great, Penny. I owe you a big thank you."

"I'm just so glad I was there. Jeez, you gave me such a scare, and all I thought was we couldn't let something weird happen here, not when we're here for *Lady Fair*. I mean, hell, I could just see the headlines. And the wagging tongues. It could turn so poisonous." They began to walk together across the lobby. "Do you want me to ride home with you? Be sure you get there all in one piece?"

"No. Actually, I'd rather you didn't. But it's all right to say something to my driver. Luke is reliable and he'll keep an eye on me." She raised a hand to stop Penny's protest. "No. Really. I'll be fine. Actually, I'd like you to go back to the party. Go back to work. The networking is important. Have a drink." She smiled. "You have a story to do. And don't forget to grab a goody bag before you leave."

Penny got her to the car where Luke had it ready at the curb. In a few words, Penny alerted Luke to what had happened. She leaned in to talk to Marge. "Take care. And I'd sure appreciate it if you call in the morning just to let me know you're okay."

"Of course, Penny. And thanks again. You've been great."

* * * *

Next morning, she was in the doctor's office. Even without Dr. Diaz's very thorough exam, including an EKG and the siphoning off of a lot of her blood, she knew what she was going to hear. She'd gotten back into her jeans, pulled on her white tee shirt and stepped, sockless, into her Manolo penny loafers. She left the examining room and went into Dr. Diaz's office, where the doctor was waiting for her. She took her seat opposite the doctor, and waited for the verdict.

For the last seven years Martine Diaz had been Marge's personal physician, and by now, Marge was familiar with this room, its furnishings and its decor. Which were the usual, mostly: a large desk, a large executive chair and two "guest" chairs, a couple of file drawers against the wall, a credenza behind the desk topped with some medical journals, professional papers, some family pictures. And a great many plants, on the window sill, on top of the file drawers, a sense of many growing things. In the examination room she'd just left, Marge had long ago reviewed the diplomas and the certificates that told the story of a first-rate education, impressive honors, and glowing recommendations—Harvard undergrad, Phi Beta and *summa cum laude,* medical school at Columbia and residencies and fellowships at prestigious universities and hospitals around the country. Specialty boards' certifications and attestations from several community organizations and official agencies—enough to choke a horse. This was a woman to respect and trust, and in these seven years, Marge had shared much of her most intimate information. She wondered how much she should tell her doctor now.

Doctor Diaz turned away from her computer. "Well, Marge. We'll have the lab results back soon and we'll see what the blood tests tell us. But I don't need a lab report to know you've been working yourself up to a collapse. You've lost twelve pounds since I saw you a couple of months ago, you're not eating right, you give every ounce of your strength and energy to that magazine, sixteen, eighteen hours a day, and you're not sleeping well. And now you've had a fainting episode. How long have I been telling you to ease up? I mean it, Marge. If you don't get a rest, you're looking for some real trouble. I'm giving you my most serious advice, and I hope the message is getting through. I know how hard it is for you to slack off a little, even when your doctor tells you you're looking for trouble if you don't." She paused, leaned back in her chair, smiled a really friendly smile, and added, "But then, what do I know? I've just been doing this for twenty years."

Marge had to laugh. She realized she'd been fighting off the truth for months, so driven by her habits of hard work, she'd stopped taking care of herself.

"I know I've been pushing really hard. But there's so much to be done, and I'm at the center of everything at *Lady Fair.* People depend on me."

"I understand, Marge. I really do. You've made yourself indispensable. But tell me, Marge," she laughed a little, "who will they all depend on after you've collapsed? Have you ever seen how fast the desk gets cleaned out after some Mr. Big Shot drops dead of overwork? He gets one day of heartfelt praise before the next guy moves in, and Mr. Big Shot is yesterday's news. I understand, your job is to run *Lady Fair.* And mine is to give you good medical care. And that includes good advice. And here's my advice. Seriously. Really seriously, Marge, I advise you to take a medical leave of absence. I want you to give yourself at least six weeks. More, if possible. Get out of town. Go somewhere where no one knows you. Or cares who you are. Someplace where they don't read *Lady Fair.* Or the *New York Post* gossip columns. Someplace pretty and quiet. No phones, no TV. Lie in the sun. Get a rest. Gain some weight. Drink piña coladas. Don't come back until you can sleep at least eight hours every night for a week." She paused, then turned and took a small framed picture from the credenza behind her. "Here. Look at this. Find yourself a place like this."

The picture looked tropical, Caribbean perhaps. Blue skies. Blue waters. Palm trees. In the distance, some simple cottages.

"Where I was born," the doctor said. "We take the kids back to the islands once a year, to see the grandparents. It's a peaceful place. Good for the soul. I recommend you find a place like this. It doesn't have to be tropical. But it has to be away from work."

Marge was surprised. Martine Diaz rarely shared personal information, though Marge knew she had a son and a daughter—their pictures were close by on the credenza, and over the years she had seen new photos being added as the kids grew. She figured they must be perhaps twelve and fifteen by now.

Marge studied her doctor's face. They weren't friends, exactly, and yet she'd always felt something simpatico between them. After all, didn't her doctor know her really well? Wasn't her whole life history buried in that computer of hers? And now her doctor was giving her important advice about managing her life. Marge was not about to ignore the advice of such a woman.

"You're right. I know you're right. It'll take a few days, at least, to arrange things. I don't want the media all over it. But I'll figure out a way."

"What about your boyfriend? Jerry? Could he go with you?"

Marge stiffened. And caught her breath. And didn't say anything.

And the doctor noticed.

"Or is Jerry part of the problem? Is he what's keeping you up at night?"

Marge couldn't decide. How much should she share with Dr. Diaz? How much was she ready to share? In a way, she owed it to the doctor and to herself to have no secrets from her if her health was involved. Before she could censor herself, she heard herself talking.

"There's someone else. Someone I knew years ago. In high school."

"Sam?"

Marge's jaw dropped.

"How did you know?"

"It's in your record here." She pointed to her computer. "At your first visit with me—seven years ago. You gave me a lot of background information and you mentioned him then, and there was something in your voice when you spoke about him. I wondered then if he'd show up again, come back into your life someday. Just a feeling I had."

This was not the first time Marge was impressed by Martine Diaz's intelligence and sensitivity. "You're very sharp, doctor. And you have an excellent memory." She glanced at the open monitor. "But I don't want you adding this to the record." Dr. Diaz turned the monitor away, and Marge nodded her thanks. "Yes, you're right. It's Sam. And I don't know if he's back in my life or not. We ran into each other a few days ago." And Marge went ahead and told her doctor about Sam's reappearance. And the emotional confusion and storm he'd started. Finishing up with, "And I guess that's what's keeping me up at night. So it's not *Lady Fair*. And I don't know if getting out of town will help."

"Oh, Marge." The doctor laughed. "It's like chicken soup," she said. "It couldn't hurt." She picked up a pen and her prescription pad, filled it out, and passed it across the desk to Marge.

Marge took it, folded it up, and put into her bag. "I'll check back with you in a few weeks," Marge said. "I'll let you know how I'm doing." Dr. Diaz walked her to the door. "Thanks again, for seeing me on a Saturday." And as she left, she added, "I'll be in touch."

In the car, as Luke drove her home, she took the prescription from her bag, unfolded it, and read:

6 weeks minimum medical leave of absence
7-8 hours of sleep every night—lights out by 10:30
3 full meals every day (plus snacks, as desired)
increase body fat by 10 pounds
1 glass red wine every day.
male company (only as desired)
zero work-related activity
and call me when you get back

Chapter Seven

She didn't tell Jerry where she was going.

"The doctor wants me to really get away, cut all ties for a couple of months. Just sit in the sun and sleep and not think about anything."

"I think it's a good idea," Jerry said. "You have been working too hard, I agree with the doc, and I'll be tied up with the case, in court every day, so it's just as well. I won't even have time to miss you. Go. Go, have a good rest. Just let me know when you're coming back."

His paperwork and his strategy sessions with co-counsel were distracting him and Marge saw that he really wasn't going to miss her. Just as well for her to be gone.

She also didn't tell him that Bridey had agreed to go along for the first few days, mainly just to help her wind down. She was glad of that because she didn't feel ready to be totally alone—not just yet. She needed a confidante.

"I know what you need," Bridey had said. "You need to start with a quiet week up at our place in Truro, up on the Cape. The summer people are gone now and you can sit on the deck and drink margaritas all day, and listen to the sound of the surf at night. It's a great place to push everything else out of your head—just watch the sea gulls and pick what's left of the blueberries. And the grapes are just coming into season now. I'll go with you, and we can talk girl talk."

"Oh, jeez, Bridey. You are the best. I know how much you really don't like to be away from your kids. If I weren't feeling so ragged, I'd never let you do this. But at least for the first few days, it really will help me not to be alone. And you're sure it's okay with Mack?"

"He'll be fine. He's a Navy man; he can handle anything. And it won't hurt me the least bit to spend a few days in the sun."

"You're a peach, Bridey. You really are. I'll just pack a few things, and I'm ready to go. I already alerted the senior staff."

"How did they take it?"

"I told them what a great job we'd done on the big issue they'd just put out, and told them I've decided to reward myself with a few weeks' vacation. Didn't say a word about 'medical' leave. What a gossip storm *that* would start! Gena Shaw's been an assistant editor long enough. She's ready to take over for a few weeks, and I advised her to put this new girl, Penny Lightly, to work. Bright girl, shows real talent and potential. I left them only an emergency call service number so I can be reached if they really need to but not to call me directly. I made it sound like I'm giving myself a few weeks of major fun, and I don't want anyone to spoil my good time."

"They'll be fine. You've trained them well."

"I hope so. I'll have my phone and Jerry can be in touch if he needs to, but he promised to let me have a real escape. And now I'm going to go and pack a bag."

"You won't need much."

"I know. I really do know how to pack light."

"I know, Marge. If there's one thing you know how to do, it's how to have the right clothes. Even when the right clothes are just a swimsuit and a towel."

"I'll stay there for a few days after you leave just to be alone to think, and then decide what I'm going to do. Then I'll come back to New York to pack up a few things, and then I'll be really gone. No one will see me till I'm ready to come home."

Chapter Eight

"I got the margaritas part right." Marge took a sip. "That's for sure. And the sun and surf are perfect too. And out there," she waved an arm toward the blue Atlantic stretching forever ahead of her, "out there, there's just the right number of sea gulls flying around." She sighed a huge sigh of contentment. "And I don't have to go blueberry-picking if I don't want to. I'm all sun screened and visored and totally comfy. I don't have to move from this spot, do I?"

Bridey laughed. "No, of course not. You don't have to move for four days. But after that, if you want to eat, you're going to have to get up and feed yourself."

"I know. You go back to New York on Tuesday, and from then on, I'm on my own."

Marge closed her eyes behind her big Givenchy sunglasses, took another sip of her margarita and sighed. There was a bowl of pretzels next to her; she took one and nibbled on it. It went well with the lime-y saltiness of the margarita. "If my doctor hadn't ordered me to gain weight, I could just lie here and not move till I totally wasted away."

Bridey did her best eye-roll. "You're supposed to rest, not die."

Marge laughed. "Don't worry. I'll eat. And I'll sleep. And maybe I'll swim a little. I might go into Provincetown, take a walk around the shops."

"Only if you promise not to look for *Lady Fair* stories. Or buy clothes for work. Or interview anyone."

"Or think about anyone."

They were both quiet for a long minute. Then Bridey said, "That's like saying 'don't think about elephants.'"

"I know."

Another long silence between them, while the gulls flew by, and the surf broke on the shore, and the sun moved just a tiny bit over from the east.

It was again Bridey who spoke first. "Are you thinking about Sam?"

"Of course."

"In a nice way?"

"Mostly."

"Whatever happened between you two?"

Marge pursed her lips, thoughtfully. She turned her face away. She loved Bridey, and she trusted her. But—

"I don't want to talk about it," she said. "Not now."

"Did Sam do something?"

"No! Oh, no! My God! No. Sam didn't do anything. You knew him, Bridey. He was always a good guy."

"Okay, Marge. Okay. I won't pry." She stood up. "I won't go poking around into your personal memories." She picked up her bag and a big oilcloth tote bag. "The cupboard is bare and I need to stock up. I'm going to drive down to Wellfleet and get some groceries. Want to come along?"

"No, thanks. I want to just lie here and think about elephants for a while. But take your cell phone. I might change my mind and decide to meet you there. We could get a coffee, maybe take a look at some of the local galleries."

"Good idea. I won't hurry back. I want to take another look at some Chinese bowls I saw at one of the gift shops. Take your time."

"I'm not running any marathons. I'll just snooze here while you're gone."

Bridey tied the ribbons of her big sun hat under her chin, slung the straps of the handbag and tote bag over her shoulders, and was gone.

* * * *

The sun was glorious. The steady roll of the surf was like a mama murmuring a lullaby. Marge had finished her drink half an hour ago, the tequila buzz hadn't yet worn off, and she thought about sleep. Maybe she could get a couple of hours lying here on the deck.

She hadn't told Bridey, but when they arrived last night, the place was so cool and quiet, and she was so exhausted, she'd thought she'd be having her first good night's rest in many weeks. But it hadn't worked out that way. The rhythmic pounding of the surf, louder it seemed in the night, was no longer a lullaby. Now it seemed to be a drum roll, commanding and portentous. The dark opened its arms to her and instead of carrying her off to dreamland, it trapped her in memories, memories that paraded, as though on a stage, the curtain of the years parted and there was Sam in a spotlight she couldn't turn off. Sam Packard, who'd been the most popular, the most charismatic boy in the school. And her own silly self, way back then, back when she was a freshman, and Sam who was a senior—imagine! A senior! She'd been so impressed with herself. All the girls were in awe. She'd been in awe herself. Yes, Bridey was right—she'd been goofy about him. Goofy, back then.

But now?

But now, he'd appeared now out of nowhere, there in the corridor at the courthouse, and she remembered everything, his voice, his eyes, and how it had been, way back then.

When they were both so young.

So she tossed all night, trying to push the memories back into their hiding place. And when the first light of morning whitened the curtains at the window, she knew she'd been through still another sleepless night. Her hands felt quivery and there was an ominous feeling of unsteadiness inside her chest as though something—a screw?—was coming loose. This had been happening for several weeks, but Dr. Diaz's tests and the lab results said she was not in danger. Not yet. And she'd learned that an hour or so of sleep would restore her to feeling normal. She was thankful at least that she was, indeed, on a vacation, and facing another day would not mean shepherding staff and content and advertisers through another issue. For the weeks ahead, at least, no one needed her, she needed no one, nothing needed to be attended to, and she refused to think about Gena Shaw and Penny Lightly and whether or not they'd be able to handle everything properly.

No! She must absolutely not think that way. She knew how to delegate effectively. She had put everything into their hands, and that's where everything would have to be until it was safe for her to return. She decided to treat herself as an employee. She gave herself instructions.

You will rest. You will not think about Lady Fair *until the doctor signs off on your medical leave. You will not return to the office until you have medical permission. You've made the necessary delegations. You will do what's necessary to preserve your health. Not only for your sake, but for the sake of the magazine. You will rest and you will have fun.*

And now, having taken herself through that drill, here on the deck, in the glorious sun and under the blue sky and with an ocean breeze cooling her, she did finally slip away into sleep and didn't move for almost two hours. She woke up smiling, and if there'd been dreams, she didn't remember what they were. She'd slept off the tequila, she was hungry, and she decided to call Bridey and see if she was still in town. Only five minutes away. She'd call and she would drive in and meet her.

* * * *

Macario's—right near the pier at Wellfleet Harbor—was not busy, now that the summer people were gone. Bridey was at a table off in a corner, and when Marge arrived, she was reading the *Cape Cod Times* and copying out a recipe for Portuguese-style pork chops onto her note pad.

"Something good?" Marge said, as she sat down.

"Sounds yummy. Too late to try it tonight; it needs to marinate a really long time. Maybe tomorrow night." She folded up the newspaper and put her note pad away. "So, did you get some rest?"

"I did. I slept for a couple of hours."

The waitress came to the table and they both ordered coffee and a platter of steamed clams to share. Macario's clams, taken out of the bay's water that very morning, were a necessity when you were in Wellfleet.

"I had a good afternoon, too." She dug into her tote bag and pulled out something wrapped in tissue paper. "I bought a set of these bowls. There's a potter here in town who makes them."

By the time they'd examined the bowls and Bridey had oohed and ahhed a bit about the great shop where she'd bought them, the clams arrived, a platter of littlenecks piled high, along with a basket of Portuguese bread, a bowl of coleslaw, a plate of butter rolls, and a bowl for the shells.

"I'm starving," Marge said. She broke off a hunk of the bread—good, plain everyday sourdough—slathered butter on it in an unladylike manner, took a big bite, and continued to talk with her mouth full. "Did you do the shopping yet? I definitely want to get some steaks. I haven't been hungry like this in many weeks. Months."

"It's the sea air."

"Right."

"It's so good for you. You'll eat. You'll sleep. You'll recharge all your batteries."

"Right."

"And then what will you do?"

"That's the thing, Bridey. I am absolutely not planning to do anything. I'm going to just put one foot in front of the other until the future rides up over the horizon. I'll think about it after you go back to town."

Marge dug into the clams, picked a shell out of the pile, held it up and lifted her face, and the clam slid out of the shell right onto her tongue, a delicate, briny young thing right out of the sea, all buttery smooth and tangy with lemon juice, a couple of chews and it slipped down her throat.

"Oh, that is so good," she said.

"You can stay up here as long as you like. Just veg out. As long as you need to. The place is yours as long as you want."

"I may stay here forever. And just eat clams." Another young clam slid down her throat.

Bridey laughed as she demolished a few clams herself. "In about ten years, Llewellyn and Henrietta may kick you out. They'll be teenagers by then and they'll be wanting to come up with their friends, and a haggard old weathered crone, which you will be by then, will get in their way. Spoil all their fun."

"Okay. I promise I'll leave by then."

"Yes. You'll have everything straightened out by then."

Marge gave her friend a good, long look.

"Yes," she said. "I'll have figured out the elephant by then."

"I sure hope so." She took her iPhone out of her bag. "But right now, I have to make a shopping list."

"Put plenty of ice cream on that list."

And there was no more talk of Marge's plans for the future.

Chapter Nine

The future had been Marge's focus ever since she was a very little girl, ever since she had clomped around the living room in her mommy's high heel shoes. And later, when she went on to stage a one-kid fashion show for her first-grade show-and-tell. Ever since that first moment, playing "dress-up," when she'd looked into the mirror and realized *I am good at this!* she understood the serious art of dress-up, that there was meaning in what we choose to wear, in what our culture tells us we must and must not wear, in fashion—high and low. In that moment, the whole universe fell into place and she knew *this is what I'm going to do!* In fourth grade, she'd created a newsletter featuring her classmates' "fashion statements." And by junior high, she'd become the go-to person for anyone—girl or boy—who needed advice about what to wear for any occasion, any event, any celebration, or, if they needed it, counseling on how to overcome fashion confusions.

She'd always known where she was headed, and the future was a path ahead of her that she'd followed as naturally as a plant turns to the light. Of course she'd written a fashion column for her high school newspaper. Of course, she went on to Parsons after high school. And of course, it was like baby to mama for her to seek her first real job at *Lady Fair.* She'd driven herself forward into her future all the years of her adult life, from the time of cutting her teeth on her first assignments, through rising to the very top of the fashion media world, putting out the kind of energy it takes to make her product the very best and to make herself the person sitting at the very top of the precarious and very competitive world she inhabited.

And now, it was time to stop. No, now it was *necessary* to stop. She'd brought herself to the point of her own imminent physical collapse. She was about to be a Looney Tunes character running frantically off the cliff, legs going furiously, until she looks down and—oh, no!—realizes she's running on thin air—and only then obeys the laws of nature and comes crashing ignominiously down to earth.

Or, to pursue that image, she was also that other cartoon character, the one who comes to a screeching stop, dug-in heels churning up ruts in the dirt.

That first image, falling to earth—that one was her own fault, wearing herself out to the point of collapse. But the second, the screeching stop—it was Sam Packard who was standing there, like a red flag, saying, "Stop, Marge. It's time to go back."

* * * *

She said nothing to Bridey. She needed to catch her emotional breath. She needed to be on a kind of mental cruise control for a few days, and just keep up the idle chatter. She needed to let the sun and the peace and quiet roll over her, and wait till Bridey returned to New York so she could be alone to think about this very new place in her life she'd come to. Bridey understood, and let her fill the few days they were together with nothing important. They sat in the sun, they cruised the gift shops, they walked around P-town in flip-flops and sun hats, with cover-ups over their swim suits, and they people-watched and ate ice cream and, because they were not tourists, they intentionally did *not* buy post cards to send out to tell the world what a great time they were having.

Until the four days had passed and it was time for Bridey to get back to Mack and the kids. Marge drove her to Provincetown's little airport, and waved goodbye to her as the little six-passenger plane fought the cross-currents off the ocean and wobbled off to Manhattan. She drove back to the house on the beach, opened up a nice dry Riesling, got out the bowl of chicken salad Bridey had left in the fridge, made a sandwich, took it all out on the deck, and got comfy with her thoughts.

Finally.

She closed her eyes and let the image of Sam Packard appear—Sam Packard as he'd appeared to her in that corridor in the courthouse—Sam Packard now a grown man, a very attractive grown man, no longer the skinny, gangly, eighteen-year-old she'd been so in love with twenty years ago. He was no longer that boy, but she remembered that boy very well. And with that memory, for the first time ever, Marge stepped off that path to the future that had been her only concern for as long as she could remember, and she allowed herself to travel down memory lane.

To a time when she felt all the power and fun of youth and was sure she knew everything she needed to know and would be able to do everything she would want to do or would need to do. To a time when friendships were casual and easy, not full of the land mines of competition and envious resentment that filled her world now. When energy was spent carelessly, as though it would always last, an endless supply like the sun, and good health could be taken for granted.

To a time when falling in love was like being washed in a radiance that created a world of its own, with its own rules and its own landscape, occupied by only the two of you, a world that excused all faults and answered all questions.

To a time twenty years ago.

* * * *

Every high school has a kid like Sam. He's the boy everyone knows. The boy everyone can get along with. The boy who breaks up every fight without taking sides. The boy who's just naturally the class president and who gets great grades without being the school genius. And who isn't exactly hot-looking, but who is not bad looking, either—though in his case, it was a near thing. He was skinny enough that every girl wanted to feed him and just casual enough about his appearance that every girl wanted to brush his hair and see how he'd look in a suit. Every girl pined for him, but no one snagged him.

And then one day, in the cafeteria, while Marge sat with her friends, spooning up a yogurt, Sam Packard stopped at her table, asked if he could join the group, said he was writing a piece for the school paper about students' career expectations, and hoped they could answer some questions about their thoughts about the future. They were a table of freshmen and they were all eager for the attention. One chair was available—the chair next to Marge—and when they all said, "Sure. Join us," he pulled it out and sat down next to her.

A strange thing happened then as his leg brushed against hers. It was just a light touch, utterly inadvertent, but it startled her. She turned to look at him—did he feel it, too? It wasn't electricity, exactly; it was too gentle for that. But something very sweet seemed to pass between them. And yes, he glanced at her and there was the tiniest bit of surprise in his expression. His eyes rested briefly on her face, as though he was making a special note of what had just passed between them. He looked away quickly.

He had a notepad and pen ready. "Okay," he said, "who wants to start?" He looked across the table to Ginny Morse and said, "How about you? Okay if I ask you a couple of questions?"

Ginny was a small girl, blond and delicate and still a little overwhelmed by actually finding herself in high school. But she was pleased to be singled out, and in a minute he had her feeling comfortable talking about herself. She had no idea about career plans—that was too far in the future—but she thought she'd like to work in an office somewhere and wear nice clothes.

"Not me," said Eleanor Mestrovic. "I've got an uncle works a farm upstate and I'm going to grow organic vegetables and sell them by the roadside, like he does. He's the happiest man I know."

"Oh, you are not," said Leigh Anders. "You'd get grubby and have dirt under your fingernails all the time, and it would be awful." Leigh was already pegged as the class snob, but she wasn't malicious so they let her sit with them. "And you'd get all sunburned and your skin would turn leathery."

Next, going around the table, he came to Bridey. She and Marge had hit it off from the first day in high school when they met in home room, discovered that they each had a goal that had been set long ago and each had decided what her future was going to be. They were immediately best friends.

"I don't think it's so awful, getting dirt under your fingernails," Bridey said. "I like hands that look like they do hard work." Sam was taking notes furiously. "I'm going to go to cooking school," Bridey said, "and I'm going to be a chef and write cookbooks and maybe own my own restaurant." She lifted her head, maybe a little defiantly, and added, "Chefs always have hands that show the marks of their work. Little burns and scrapes and cuts. On the cooking shows on TV, look at their hands. Hard-working hands. I like that."

"That's true," Carrie Kim said. "Like dancers. Have you any idea what a ballet dancer's feet look like inside those toe shoes? I'm going to be a dancer, if I'm good enough, and I know what toe work does to your feet. It's part of the job, and you just do it, if you love what you're doing."

Leigh and Carrie started to argue about how much physical or cosmetic damage a woman should bear for the sake of her work, but Sam intervened.

"I think I know what Marge here thinks she's going to do." She was surprised that he knew her name. And her face showed her surprise. "Yes," he said. He was looking at her as though he already knew her well. Almost as though they were –what?—already friends? "I read the piece you submitted to the paper," he said. "About fashion and girls in high school. And how a girl could look super cool and smart without having to spend a fortune. I was really impressed." Every girl at the table turned to look at Marge.

"I don't see how Marge gets away with it," Leigh said. "Every day, she comes up with the weirdest outfits. I mean, look at what she's wearing today. It's great, Marge. Really. It's a talent. And we all love you for it, but honestly! Every day. The weirdest outfits!"

It was true. Every day was something brand new and sometimes just barely this side of comical. Or, if not comical, then dramatic, or theatrical, or just plain outrageous. Today it was a man's white shirt, a man's tie, cropped black pants, and an oversize gold-brocaded vest.

"It's my Annie Hall look," she said. She turned and looked at Sam directly. "Do you like it?"

"I actually do. I like it a lot." He really had the nicest smile.

"And you think you know what I'm planning to be doing when I 'grow up'?"

"I do. I'd bet you think you're going to be the editor in chief of *Lady Fair*. Someday."

"Not someday. By the time I'm thirty."

"By the time you're thirty? Really? You sure aim high," he said. He was writing it all down. "But in the meantime, to help you get there, how about you come and work on the school paper? We need good writers, and it's a great bunch of guys. We can use someone like you."

The girls around the table were clearly impressed.

"Could I write a fashion column?"

Now he studied her even more carefully. "That would be something new in our paper," he said. "Do you think you'd be able to produce a column a month?"

"Yes, of course."

"Then we'll try you out." He thought for a moment and then said, "If it works, we'll call your column 'The Clothes Horse.' Can you get your first piece to me by a week from today?"

"I can get it to you tomorrow."

"You're very sure of yourself, aren't you?"

She just smiled. And he smiled back at her.

* * * *

They worked well together on the paper. She saw him regularly in staff meetings, and strategy sessions. She always turned in her column two weeks before publication, and it became one of the most popular columns in the paper. Sam teased her regularly about her wild outfits, but he was funny and not mean-natured and she enjoyed the attention.

Within a month, he'd asked her out. They were in a small school in a small town, so everyone soon knew that Sam Packard, a senior, was dating Marge Webster, who was only fourteen and a freshman. The comments were good-natured, because Sam was liked by everyone. And he was dating other girls, too. But still—

Sam's response was to insist that Marge was a very interesting girl, and anyway, he'd be going away to college in the fall, so they were just friends and he thought she was fun.

But for her part, Marge was sure she was in love. At fourteen, it's so easy to fall in love. Look at Romeo and Juliet. Weren't they just teenagers? If they were alive today, the story would probably have been different. No one would have been forcing her to marry an old man, and a month or so later, Romeo would have gotten interested in some other girl, or Juliet would have dumped him and taken up with someone else—Mercutio, maybe, if he weren't such a hothead and got himself killed.

Anyway, Marge was fourteen and in love—'goofy,' as Bridey said— and no one knew what Sam was really thinking because he kept his more serious thoughts to himself. Marge wasn't sensitive enough to notice the signs, the way he was careful of her, careful of her feelings, careful to keep them both from getting too seriously passionate, respectful of the fact that she was, after all, only fourteen. She noticed but didn't understand what it meant that he paid attention to everything she said, with an indulgent gentleness in his expression while she ranted on about what was fashionable and what was not, and about her writing and her future in journalism and all the great things she was going to do. She didn't realize that her plans for her future seemed pretty juvenile to him, but he would never have tried to shoot her down. He figured she'd outgrow all that stuff about being an editor in chief by thirty. Maybe someday she'd be on the staff of some fashion magazine, but editor in chief of *Lady Fair?* The premier fashion magazine in the world? Little girl from a little upstate town? Not likely.

Well, Sam, at eighteen, was young, too.

But he'd be going away in the fall and he wasn't ready to make any real plans. He'd decided to major in political science and thought he might be going into politics. Or something related. Nothing definite yet. So he wasn't about to make any long-term declarations.

But in April, when her birthday came around, he went to her birthday party and he gave her a necklace. It was a thin silver chain with a little silver charm in the form of a pony, and he'd written on the card "Happy Birthday to our school's Clothes Horse." She meant to wear it forever but at just-turned-fifteen, "forever" is a notion that is little understood.

* * * *

A week later, Sam asked her to his senior prom. Marge was absolutely puffed up with pride and excitement, and she took it as proof that there could be something serious between them.

"You lucky thing!" Bridey said. "What are you going to wear?"

"Oh, I'll figure out something. I haven't decided yet. Something traditional? You know, like a classic prom dress? Or something really special no one would think to wear to a prom? Black jeans and a ruffled shirt. Or a bikini top."

Bridey laughed. "You'll come up with something."

"I know."

She didn't need to think about the dress. No, deciding on the right dress was the easy part. Fashion was, after all, Marge's medium, and if there was anything she understood, it was how to make interesting and effective wardrobe choices to honor the event, to express her personality and her moods, her sense of the time and place. What worried her were the butterflies in her stomach. She knew she'd be among Sam's classmates, boys and girls older than herself by three years, and she worried that she'd make some sort of mistake, do something stupid, make a fool of herself. And embarrass Sam in front of his friends, in front of the whole senior class. Usually, self-confidence was one of Marge's strong suits, but on this occasion, for goodness' sake, the senior prom!—well, it would be a test of her maturity.

About the dress, she decided, finally, on an absolutely plain black silk sheath with spaghetti straps, and no accessory other than a long string of pearls and pearl earrings. And on the evening of the prom, when she checked out every detail in the tall three-way mirror in her bedroom, she felt exquisitely grown-up and elegant. Surely, Sam would see that she was mature enough, even at fifteen, to make plans beyond his graduation. She hoped there'd be something promised between them before he went away in the fall.

But when the time came, the evening turned out differently from everything she'd expected. And it wasn't Sam's fault. Sam did all the right things. He arrived right on time, in his old, beat-up Mazda. He came to the front door, in a conventional black tux and bow tie, and he shook hands with Marge's dad and promised her mom they'd be home by midnight. A week earlier, he'd surreptitiously and very delicately quizzed Bridey about Marge's dress and so he brought the perfect corsage—a plain and very lovely cluster of small calla lilies, which he fastened around her wrist. He was clearly impressed by the sophistication of the dress she'd chosen, and he meant it when he told her she looked really beautiful. When they got to the car, he held the door for her to help her into the front seat. With Sam as her escort, all her anxieties disappeared.

The evening went well. Great, in fact. Sam and several other couples had rented a room at the town's only hotel, and they started the evening there, drinking beer and eating pretzels and dancing and—a little bit, some of them—making out, in a genteel and tentative way. Marge had never liked beer, so she stuck to the pretzels and Sam was not a boy to join in the nuzzling publicly, nor would he let any girl he was with be compromised—especially a girl as young as Marge—so they just danced and revved themselves up for the evening. After about an hour, they left to go to the school's gym where the prom was happening. Turned out, the music was good, the buffet food was well done, the mock cocktails were drinkable, and all their friends were there, so they remained until eleven when the festivities were officially shut down. Marge had been having a good time and she hadn't disgraced herself or Sam. His friends accepted her with no problems, especially since they all knew her work for the newspaper, which made her a little bit of a celebrity at school. She expected to go back to the room where the post-prom party was continuing, but Sam surprised her. He said he wanted to spend the rest of the evening alone with her. "Let's go to Spatz's," he said. "Where we can talk."

Spatz's Diner was the only place in town that stayed open all night. And if Sam wanted to be alone to talk, Marge felt this was portentous. Maybe, she hoped, he wanted to talk about them, and maybe about their future? This was more interesting, more exciting, than any post-prom party where they'd all be drinking more, making out more, and maybe getting her involved in ways she wasn't ready to get into—not just yet.

They got settled at their table, ordered Cokes and nachos, and under the table, Marge had her fingers crossed.

"I wanted to talk to you because I won't be seeing you for the rest of the summer."

Marge's heart fluttered.

"I'll be leaving in a few days," he said. "The family's taking a road trip out west and we won't be back till the end of the summer. And then, when we get back, the plan is for me to leave right away for school. So tonight is our last chance to be together."

"I didn't know you'd be leaving so soon. I thought we'd be seeing each other before you left." Inside, she was pleading. *Not so soon!! Not yet! Please don't go away now!* Under the table, she uncrossed her fingers and put her hands on the table. She needed to do something with them. She scooped up a chip loaded with cheese and guacamole. "I'll miss you, Sam. School won't be the same without you." She ate the chip. She felt as though she was going to cry.

"Hey," Sam said. "I want to stay in touch, Marge. We can write to each other. And I'll be back in town for holidays. Harvard isn't so far away. The thing is, this is a big move for me, and a really big opportunity to build my future. Whatever that's going to be. I need to really concentrate. Focus my energies. Don't let myself get sidetracked. "

What Sam was saying was that he was becoming a man. What Marge heard was "goodbye." She felt as though he were dismissing her. She wanted to say, "*I can be part of your future, Sam.*" But maybe he'd think she was being silly. She'd started out the evening feeling so grown up, and here were all her fantasies crumbling around her. It hit her really hard that she wasn't old enough to be taken seriously, to be a part of any man's life. Not yet. She felt ashamed. She looked away, fighting off the tears. What an awful way to end the evening, an evening that was supposed to be so special!

Sam took her hand. "Hey, come on, Marge. I bet you have a great future ahead of you, too. Maybe you'll do important things, too."

Somehow, that made her angry. As though he were patronizing her.

"That's right." She could feel herself digging in her heels, determined not to let his condescension humiliate her further. She had always sensed that behind his good-natured teasing, he really didn't take her plans seriously. "That's right," she repeated, more forcefully. She raised her head, felt her neck stiffen. "Yes, Sam. I'm going to do great things."

"Right." He was laughing now. "I know. You're going to be the editor in chief of *Lady Fair* magazine. Before you're thirty."

He was laughing, but she wasn't. She was mad.

"I will be. You'll see."

She pulled her hand out of his, but he took it back again. More seriously, he said, "Marge, it's good to have goals, aim high and all that. I know. But I hate to see the way you're setting yourself up to be disappointed. Sometimes people have to settle for more realistic goals. That's not a bad thing. Honestly, honey. Don't set yourself up to get hurt."

I just did, she thought. *I set myself up with you, and I won't make that mistake again.*

"Okay," she said. She could feel herself pulling away from Sam. Sam, who was such a good guy, but who couldn't take her seriously. Sam, who was leaving to go to Harvard to build his brilliant career, doing whatever it was going to be.

I'm going to go on and build my own brilliant career, and you can go to hell, Sam Packard. Everyone's darling boy. Well, you're not my darling boy.

"I suppose you're right," she said, taking another chip, and scooping up a bit of the sour cream. "It's silly to aim so high. After all, who do I think I am? The Queen of Sheba?" She chomped down the chip and took another one. "So tell me more about your plans for Harvard. What are you expecting?"

"Now you're mad," he said. "I didn't mean to make you mad. Really. I just want you to be sensible."

"Well, Sam." She was feeling even more stiff-necked now. "I really don't need you to teach me how to feel sensible. I'm a very sensible person. I have my plans, too. And don't I do good work for the school paper? Don't I write a good column? Doesn't everyone tell you how much they like it? Isn't it always delivered on time—no, ahead of time. Don't I have all the makings of a really good journalist? And don't I really know my subject? Do you know anyone who knows as much about fashion as I do? And don't I—"

"Whoa, there. Slow down. It's true, you write a really good column. So good, in fact, I've recommended you for editor of the paper next year. Hadn't had a chance to tell you yet, but it will get approved, of course, and the job is yours beginning in September." He didn't wait for her to say thank you, which she was about to do, grudgingly, considering how angry she was. "But let's face it. You and I both know fashion is not exactly rocket science. It's not earthshaking news if hemlines go up or down. You know that. Or if 'they' are wearing fur or felt this year. It's not a thing any sane person can take totally seriously. And for you to get your whole life—I mean your *whole* life—tied up in it, your whole ego, all your passion and intelligence committed to what women are wearing, well Marge, honey. It's just plain dumb!"

That did it.

She stood up.

"Take me home, Sam."

He stood up, too. "Now listen, honey. There's no need—"

"Don't call me 'honey.' You don't know me well enough for that. Just take me home."

And she headed for the door.

Sam dropped a bunch of bills on the table and ran after her.

Now he was mad, too.

"You're acting like a little girl," he said. "I thought you were more mature than that."

Nothing he could have said would have been more wrong than that.

Neither one of them spoke another word all the way back to her home. He pulled up in front of her house. She got out immediately and stalked up the driveway. He drove away as soon as she was inside the front door.

* * * *

He wrote to her a couple of times that summer, to tell her he was sorry, to explain how he really felt about her. But she was still mad and still hurt and she tore up his letters without reading them and threw them away.

And in September, Sam went off to Harvard, and Marge became the school newspaper's first female editor, and they didn't see each other again.

Until twenty years later, when they bumped into each other on a Friday evening, in the corridor of a courthouse on Centre Street in Manhattan.

Chapter Ten

For five days, Marge finished up the food Bridey had left for her, ate lots of ice cream, drank margaritas, white wine, and buckets of iced tea and stared out over the ocean, thinking, remembering, planning. By the end of the five days, she knew what she was going to do, how she would do what Martine Diaz's prescription ordered her to do. And it wasn't going to be soaking up the sunlight there on a deck staring out over the dunes of Cape Cod and counting sea gulls. Or baking under a tropical sun in the Caribbean, either.

On the morning of the sixth day, she closed up the house, notified Bridey that it would be vacant, "just in case Llewellyn and Henrietta wanted to use it." She called for a cab to take her to Provincetown's airport, and by eleven a.m. she was in the air, and as soon as she got back to New York, she texted Jerry.

I'm home. Cn u get away 4 dinner?

How's the case going?

The answer came right back.

In court now. this one's a bitch. but quick dinner's okay. Brahma House?

7:30 p.?

The Brahma House was near Jerry's office, so she knew his time was tight. Probably he'd have just enough time to eat and then get back to work.

Just as well. She expected this dinner to go quickly, and she didn't want to have to tell him not to come to her place afterwards. If this case was preoccupying him, he'd probably just as soon go to his own apartment. Or even sleep on the sofa in his office, which he sometimes did. Also, Brahma House was a good choice. It was one of those quiet, elegant, intimate places where the service was perfect, the food was impeccable, and tables far enough apart so it was possible to talk without being overheard—and without overhearing the neighbors.

She spent the rest of the afternoon packing. She wasn't going to need much. No one would be seeing her twice. Jeans and tee shirts mostly. Good walking shoes. A short trench coat in case of rain, with a removable lining as the weather was getting chillier. A denim jacket. A pretty chiffon dress from Dolce & Gabbana, a print of pink, gray and black peonies, if she needed something a bit dressy. And chiffon would pack easily. No jewelry except a plain watch—the old Timex she'd had since she was in school—and pearl earrings. And that was about it. The necessary lingerie and toiletries. And big dark sunglasses, to help her hide if she needed to. It all went into a single carry-on. Notebook and passport in her handbag. A paperback to read on the plane. Several pens. No electronic devices, except her phone.

Perfect. All done in under an hour. Including the long minute she stood there in the middle of her bedroom, with her carry-on open on the bed, with the small purple velvet jewelry pouch in her hand, while she decided that yes, it should go along with her. And tucked it down into one of the inside pockets of her carry-on bag.

After the bag was packed, she set it near the door. Then she got settled comfortably on her sofa with her laptop set onto the coffee table in front of her. She logged in and quickly located some small, out-of-the-way hotels, made reservations, and then booked her airline tickets. Economy class only. She deliberately didn't use *Lady Fair's* travel department, and charged all to her personal credit card. With that taken care of, it was time to leave to meet Jerry.

* * * *

She loved the Brahma House restaurant. It was always unobtrusive. It suited her mood perfectly. She planned to have a nice talk with Jerry, explain what was happening, and then leave directly for the airport. Her flight was a red eye and she'd be able to make it to the airport in time for her midnight flight.

Jerry was already there when she arrived, and the maître d' took her directly to their table, where Jerry was studying some papers. He leaned over to kiss her as she sat down, and said, "I'm glad you're back. Did you have a good rest?"

"I sat in the sun, I ate lots of clams and ice cream, and drank margaritas, and I got some sleep. But not enough. And I want to talk to you about that." She paused to look at the menu, decided on the scallops, took a bit of flatbread from the basket and nibbled on it. "This case is keeping you busy?"

"It's a tough one. It's good to get away from it for a little while. Let's not even talk about it." He slipped the papers he'd been looking at into the case he'd set on the floor next to him. "It's keeping the whole team up late every night."

"Then you won't mind at all if I'm away for a few weeks?"

"Probably just as well. I'm not going to be good company while this is going on."

She knew how he got when a case was troubling him. Distracted. Preoccupied. Grumpy. Might as well be a hundred miles away. On a distant planet.

"Then you won't mind."

She could see him bringing his mind around to setting aside what he'd been working on and focusing on her.

"Won't mind what?"

"Doctor's orders. You've been right, telling me I was driving myself too hard. Dr. Diaz says I have to get away. At least several weeks. So I'm just going to take off—disappear—be incommunicado. I don't want anyone to know where I am—and don't get mad, Jerry, but that means you, too. I just need to know that no one knows where I am, so I can really rest. I'm packed. I'm leaving tonight. I've made all the arrangements and told them at the office that I'm giving myself a vacation—but no one at *Lady Fair* will know where I am, either."

Jerry sat back and looked thoughtfully at her, for a long minute.

"Suppose there's an emergency?" he said.

She took a card from her bag and handed it to him.

"Here's an emergency contact number, and I've given it to them at the office, too. If it really is necessary, I can be reached. But I mean it, Jerry. Only if it's really necessary. Totally incommunicado!"

"You'll be all right?"

"Of course I'll be all right. I'll just be out of touch. That's all. And I'll be resting, taking it easy, giving myself no problems. It'll be good for me."

He shook his head thoughtfully, thinking it over. Then he said, "Okay, then." He picked up the menu. "Have you decided?"

"I'll have the scallops," she said. Jerry said he'd have the same and signaled the waiter who came and took their order along with Jerry's choice from the wine list, a bottle of a nice Vouvray that he knew was one of Marge's favorites.

"To wish you have a good rest," he said, by way of a toast, with glass lifted toward her, "and that you enjoy your vacation. And to tell you that I'll miss you."

And that was that. She felt she'd gotten over a difficult hurdle and was glad Jerry wasn't making a fuss about her being away. From there on, the subject shifted and they talked about trivia. The weather on Cape Cod, and whether her flight down was uneventful—Jerry hated those tiny planes, but she thought they were cute—and what to do about his secretary who'd forgotten, again, to renew one of his magazine subscriptions.

They were eating their scallops and drinking their wine when a group of diners at a table in the far corner apparently finished their dinner and got up to leave. Four men, finishing what appeared to be a business dinner. They all looked serious and thoughtful, and seemed to have weighty matters on their well-coiffed heads. On the way to the door, they passed Marge's table. One of the men stopped, said to the others, "You go on back to the office. I'll catch up with you later."

Neither Marge nor Jerry had noticed that Jerry's opposing counsel, Sam Packard, and his team of co-counsel had, like them, chosen to have dinner that night at the Brahma House. But with Sam pausing at their table, he had to acknowledge that he and his adversary were all there together.

An awkward moment for Marge. To say the least.

But the two men were cool and professional. These chance meetings were not so unusual in the downtown financial district around the courthouses and in the rather rarefied restaurants they frequented, and they both knew how to leave the courtroom behind them when they met socially.

"Nice to see you again, Marge," he said. "And you, too, Jerry. A lot more pleasant here than where we were this afternoon." He smiled at Marge. "Your boyfriend here gave me a hell of a run today. Your cross of our last witness, Jerry, that was tough. We'll be up late tonight handling that one."

"We aim to please, Sam." Jerry shook his head at the praise; he knew it for the "aw shucks" ploy that it was. He knew he'd hardly laid a glove on that witness. "But you had him well-prepared."

Sam said to Marge, "Have you ever seen Jerry at work in court?"

"A couple of times. I usually don't understand what's going on." She hoped her voice sounded normal. She was feeling completely at sea, with these two men being so cordial with each other.

And then Jerry said, "Listen, Sam. Would you like to join us? Have a glass of wine. It's a nice white from the Loire. And you and Marge can catch up a little."

Sam looked toward the door and saw that the other men had already left. He seemed to give it a quick thought, and then said, "I don't want to interrupt your dinner." Why did that sound like a "yes"?

"No problem. That's okay with you, Marge. Isn't it?"

What could she say?

"Of course. Please join us."

He looked once more toward the door. "Okay," he said. "They won't need me for a little while." He pulled over a chair from a nearby table. And laughed. "Ten minutes, anyway." The waiter came and poured a glass for him. He held it up as though for a toast. "Here's to old times," he said. He turned to Marge and very seriously he added, "It really is good to see you again, Marge."

She felt she must be blushing. Or turning very pale. Something. It wasn't possible for anyone to be as nervous as she felt without something showing on her face.

"How long has it been?" Jerry asked. "Since high school?"

Together, they both said, "Twenty years."

And they both laughed.

"I wish I'd known Marge back then," Jerry said. "Has she changed much?"

Sam looked her over, as though examining something very special.

"Yes, I think she's changed." Then he gave Marge a big smile. "Can I tell him, Marge?"

"I don't see why not. I don't remember anything too awful." This was like a test. Was Sam Packard still the good guy, the honorable guy she remembered from twenty years ago?

"I have to tell you, Jerry. She seems all grown up now. But she was such an oddball back then. Every day, she was in the most outrageous get-ups. Or the most interesting. Or the most beautiful. You never knew, one day to the next, what it would be. But it was clear that she was trying out all the different personalities that clothes could express. Did she tell you, Jerry? She started out writing a fashion column for our school newspaper. It was a terrific column, the highest rated of everything in the paper. And then, after I left, she was its editor in chief. There was no question, the fashion world was where she was going to wind up." Then he looked so fondly at Marge, even Jerry had to notice. "But you said you were going to be *Lady Fair's* editor in chief by the time you were thirty, and you really did get to do it. Your dreams were so big, so very big for such a young girl."

"Most people at school didn't think I could do it."

"You proved us all wrong."

"You didn't think I could do it, back then."

"No, actually, I didn't."

"I remember."

"I do, too. And I'm sorry. I owe you an apology."

She was silent for a moment. Then she said, "I owe you one, too."

"So," he said. "Are we even, now?"

"I don't know."

Even Jerry realized he was outside this conversation. They were talking about something that was not being shared with him.

Marge looked at her watch. She stood up abruptly. "Listen, you guys. This little jaunt down memory lane has been great, but I have a plane to catch. Sam, it was good to see you again. And Jerry, I'll let you know before I get back."

The two men stood up, too. They both looked surprised by the suddenness of her move.

"Where are you going?" Sam asked.

"Not telling. Just giving myself a vacation for a few weeks." And she collected her carry-on from the coat check and she was gone.

Jerry and Sam looked at each other. Jerry said, "No need for you to go. Finish your wine."

And Sam said, "A vacation?"

"She's been working too hard. She needs a rest."

Sam looked very thoughtfully at Jerry, as though measuring him. "She was always a little odd. Hard to understand."

Jerry was measuring Sam right back. "Not with me, she's not," he said.

"Well, then. That answers your question. She really has changed."

They stared at each other for a long minute. A very long minute.

Then Jerry said, "Sam, I want to marry that woman."

"So did I, once." Sam lifted his glass. He made a little gesture with it, an acknowledgement that he and Jerry were adversaries in ways beyond the courtroom, and drank it down. "I'll see you in court, tomorrow morning."

And he left.

Chapter Eleven

In her window seat, buckled up and coach-class anonymous, Marge took one long, settling-down deep breath and prepared herself for takeoff as the plane taxied to the runway. She had made this trip hundreds of times, yet still, in these moments of the grumbling, growling, still earth-bound ride along the tarmac, she always felt as though the great giant that carried her was gathering its strength, preparing to perform its stunningly impossible feat. There was the pause as it turned onto the runway, the positioning of itself as the plane seemed to take a preparatory breath, and then there was the gathering roar and the huge machine did the magnificent, improbable magic of leaving the earth and taking itself and its passengers up and up and up some six miles or more into the nighttime sky, to cross an entire ocean, with an admiring moon just off to the right ahead of them. No matter how many times Marge made this trip, no matter how much work she was prepared to do while making the crossing, or how occupied she was with the chatter of a traveling companion, there were always these first moments as the plane rose up into the sky that filled her with excitement, admiration, and wonder at the improbability of the entire event.

And this time, as she glanced around her, it added to her pleasure to know that no one knew who she was, or knew what she was doing there. The elderly woman, white-haired and tiny, sitting in the middle seat next to her, was writing some lines into a notebook, a diary, perhaps. In the aisle seat a bearded, long-legged young man struggled to fit himself into the cramped space while setting big, high tech looking headphones over his ears. Not since her rookie days had Marge traveled coach and she enjoyed the sense that she was traveling in disguise. She closed her eyes, slipped a sleep mask over her face, took a deep, deep breath, and told herself not to wake up until they landed at Heathrow.

"Thank God!" She almost said it aloud. "I escaped them all."

She felt like a kid again.

* * * *

It was the best sleep she'd had in weeks, and the landing was so soft, she felt as though the pilot had been careful to waken her as gently as possible. It seemed to signal that her recovery was now truly beginning. All around her, passengers were checking their phones, letting friends and relatives know they'd arrived. At the gate, she watched the first-class people leave the plane and was so thankful that this time there'd be no reporters waiting for her, no car waiting to take her to the Berkeley Square offices of *Lady Fair* in Mayfair, no rush of activity to demand every tiniest bit of her energy and attention. Around her, passengers were pulling their carry-ons down from the overhead, already crowding into the aisles, some of them rushing to make a connection, others just rushing to get off and hurry into their busy schedules.

Marge had no need to rush—indeed, she wasn't *allowing* herself to rush—so she waited in her seat until the plane was almost empty. Then she collected her carry-on and left to take the long walk to the taxi stand outside the terminal. She waited her turn for a taxi, gave the driver the address of a place she'd found online, a small hotel just off Bayswater Road, opposite Kensington Gardens. An out-of-the way place, grand in an old-fashioned way and off any track beaten by anyone who was likely to know her or recognize her.

It was a lovely morning, a little misty in a nice London sort of way, the fog not yet burned off, with early-morning traffic into the city just beginning to gather. She realized that this was the first time she'd made this ride from the airport without being busy with work obligations, and she was able to just look around her. She saw how much had changed since she'd made her first wide-eyed visit, back in her Parsons school days. She'd been so young back then, making her first trip abroad and so eager to see everything. But the years and the work had changed her and she'd lost that freedom to just sponge up every new sight, every new experience.

Oh, this was going to be a really new phase in her life.

She peered out at the passing scene, feeling so young again.

And she thought of Sam.

She tried not to. She told herself that if anyone should be here with her, it should be Jerry. But what could she do? There was Sam, insisting on being her companion on this adventure, insisting on showing her a good time. Crowding Jerry out.

"No!"

"Yes, luv?" said the driver. He tipped his head back to hear her.

She'd said it aloud, and she was embarrassed.

"Sorry. No, it's okay."

Talking to myself. I really do need a rest!

The driver returned his attention to the road, and she kept her thoughts to herself. Thoughts that continued to be about Sam.

This isn't good. Not fair to Jerry.

She tried. She really did. But it was Sam who kept coming back. Sam who looked out of the window with her, and enjoyed what was happening to the old city. Sam who would get a kick out of the way new footprints were being placed over the ancient ones. Who would like that the old and the new were living together. Jerry would have complained that traditions were being trashed. Marge wasn't sure which way she leaned.

If she was going to rest and recuperate, this wrangle inside her was going to have to stop! She forced herself to watch the view through the window, to *not* think about Jerry or Sam or all the nifty things she could be doing at Berkeley Square, and to just get herself settled into the quiet little room she'd taken in the quiet old hotel, where no one knew her, where there was nothing to do but eat and sleep and get her system back in shape.

* * * *

The lobby of the old hotel, built in the time of King Edward VII, was exactly as its online photo showed it—with dark woods and high-coffered ceilings, grand chandeliers, great displays of fresh flowers, and an elaborately carved receptionist's desk. No elevator—a broad marble staircase winding up to the floors above. Marge's room turned out to be just as pictured, tiny but comfortable, well-lit and well-appointed. It would be her nest away from home. She needed nothing more.

After a quick shower and change of jeans and tee shirt, she went down to the dining room, had a leisurely breakfast of bacon and eggs, and then headed out into the sunlight. She paused at the top of the stone steps down to the street, blinking a little in the light, and looked right and left, deciding which way to go. This was a part of London she didn't know at all, but she'd picked up a map at the concierge's desk so she couldn't get lost, and she was ready to go exploring. She went down the short flight to the street, let her feet choose for her and walked to the left. Then left again at the corner, and right and left, walking at random, enjoying the neighborhood feel of the streets, no tall buildings here, only small shops and rows of sedate residences, even a Starbucks, and all peaceful. So different from the quick pace of New York. She knew it would be good for her here. She would get better, she'd get her health back, she'd get her sanity back, and she'd stop the adolescent mooning about a high school romance.

She'd walked perhaps a half hour, checked the street sign at the nearest corner, and discovered she was on Portobello Road. The name was, of course, familiar to her. Everyone has heard of Portobello Road. But in all her many trips to London, she'd never actually had the time to visit this legendary antique and used clothing market. She'd expected something much broader but discovered a long, narrow street, crowded with racks of clothes and food stalls and antique shops, an everyday version of the street fairs familiar on summer weekends in New York. It was a lazy stroll she made, pausing to check out the racks of clothing, reminding herself that she was not working, that she was only a tourist, getting a good long rest from the usual grind. The crowding of people and stalls and racks of clothes thinned out toward the street's northern end and she turned back, retracing her steps. She bought a falafel from a street vendor and ate it as she walked along. She felt happy. Sunlight, food, and no obligations—surely this was the best medicine.

She meandered back in the general direction of her hotel and found herself walking along Bayswater Road, with Kensington Gardens to her right. At the Black Lion Gate, she went into the park and wandered about for another hour.

But why follow her through the rest of the day? Or even the next few days? There is no need. This stay in London was only the first phase in Marge's plan for her rest and recovery, and it was a very easy plan for her to follow. In fact, she'd decided to have no plan at all and to simply walk and walk and walk, with no agenda and no expectations. To soak up the city and to see it in ways she never had before. To keep the pressures of her work at bay by not letting anyone be in touch with her for several weeks. And to think only happy thoughts. And this is what she was doing, these next days, just walking and walking and walking, exploring sections of the city that were totally unfamiliar to her, sections that were far from the usual tourist sites. Far from *Lady Fair* and Berkeley Square and the runway venues and the celebrity parties. She was eating foods she'd never tried before. And people-watching in a way she'd not had time for in years, imagining the lives of folks who passed her in the street, or who sat nearby in the park, or were overheard in restaurants, on a bus, imagining their homes, their families, their occupations. Looking beyond their clothes. Looking beyond how her magazine could use their stories, their possible acclaim, their noteworthiness.

And gradually she was getting healthier. Which did not mean that the rigid discipline of her adult life had yet returned. Not at all. In fact, all the solitude and freedom from pressure allowed her mind to go wherever it wanted, and it seemed that her mind insisted on going back to that other time in her life, when she was so much younger, and when a crush on a boy could seem to define her very being, and when she hadn't yet the mature self-control that had forced her to move on from Sam.

Sam. Sam Packard. There it was. With all her walking and trying new foods and looking at London's great diversity of people and the multiplicity of their lives, she was unable to keep Sam from accompanying her. He was there with her, whatever she did and wherever she went. She found herself mentally sharing with him each new experience, each new sight, and imagining his responses, their shared interest, their shared pleasure. She scolded herself, but it did no good. There he was.

It was on her fifth day in London, a Saturday, that everything got turned upside down.

The day started well enough. As had become her custom, she had breakfast in the hotel's dining room, scones and jam and coffee and a bowl of berries, and then went out onto the steps to the street. As usual, she had no plan for the day and let her feet take her wherever they would. This morning, they took her toward Kensington Gardens where, instead of going inside, she walked left on Bayswater and continued on all the way to the Hyde Park corner. The day was cool, with some overhanging clouds, and she wondered if she should have brought an umbrella. *Well, if it rains, I can always duck into a pub or a cafe to sit it out—there are coffee shops everywhere.* This was one of the perks of her uncommitted days, of being free to check out at any time.

She walked all the way to the east end of the park, to Marble Arch, and decided to go on into the park and spend an hour or so strolling, people-watching, observing this or that interesting bit of the passing scene. She'd bought a *Times* earlier, and maybe, if it didn't rain, she might sit on a bench and read her paper. Or watch children playing in the park. She smiled, with some guilt, because there was Sam, her imagined companion, right along with her, enjoying the day, enjoying her comments, enjoying her pleasure.

But she'd gone barely a hundred feet when a crowd at Speakers' Corner caught her attention. It was an animated bunch, almost all men, some cheering and some yelling and jeering at the speaker whose harangue she couldn't at all make out. She was amused by all their passion, cheerers and jeerers alike, and she paused to watch. This was more fun than sitting on a bench and watching children play. The crowd was animated, yes, and it was all very interesting even if she couldn't figure out what it was about. But then, after maybe five minutes or so, the crowd's energy around her was increasing. The tone changed from energy to agitation to real anger, and as she tried to make out what was going on, what issues were so enraging the people around her, she realized that more and more people were arriving. The crowd was getting bigger and noisier and angrier. In fact, the crowd's fury was escalating and it was beginning to feel—well—menacing? And she finally realized that she might actually be in danger. At first, she told herself to calm down, that she was in a perfectly lovely park in London and nothing awful was going to happen.

But then a genuine fight broke out only a few feet away from her, and fists were flying. Someone stepped hard on her foot, an elbow jabbed her sharply in the back, and she was bring pushed about by the press of the crowd. She knew she had to get away. But how to get out of this mass of bodies, these waving arms and clenched fists and furious faces?

Then suddenly a hand gripped her arm. At first, she was about to fight it off, to resist its pull on her, but a firm voice close to her ear said, "Let's get you out of here!" and a strong arm was clearing a path for her among the frenzied bodies. She was holding up her newspaper to shield her face, afraid of the crowd's attack, so it wasn't until they were clear of the roiling mass of bodies and out onto a clear space of grass, that she saw the face of the man who'd rescued her, who'd just turned to her and said, "Are you all right?"

She thought, for a moment, that someone in the crazy riot she'd just come out of must have hit her on the head and knocked her brains askew. Her eyes, as they say, were deceiving her. She couldn't make sense of what she was seeing.

"Sam?"

What could she do but stare at him?

"You're all right?" he asked again.

She had no answer. Had she been knocked silly? Was she in London? Or in New York? Was this Sam? Or someone who looked a lot like him?

She shook her head—as though to clear it.

"Oh, jeez," he said. "I must have surprised you, just showing up like that."

Now she caught her breath. A little. That was certainly Sam's voice.

"Surprised me?" she said. "Well, yes. You surprised me. You sure did. A little bit more than surprised. I thought I'd lost my mind." She blinked a couple of times, as though that would help her think. "I can't breathe."

"Hey, let's find you a place to sit down." He looked around. "Over there," he said, pointing. He took her arm again, gently this time. The riot seemed to have settled down a bit, the police had arrived and were arresting people, and no one paid any attention as he led her to a nearby bench. "I guess I should explain," he said.

"Yes, I guess you should."

They sat down together on the bench.

"They told me at the hotel that you had just left, so I came out and saw you walking down Bayswater Road. I thought it would be fun to surprise you, so I just followed you till you came into the park. When you stopped to watch the speech, I was going to wait till you moved on. I didn't want to surprise you right in the middle of all those people. And then the crowd got nasty and I saw you were in a bad spot." He looked at her seriously. "I was really scared for you, Marge."

She didn't even know where to start. "But what are you doing in London? Why aren't you in New York? What about the litigation? With Jerry? Has it settled? And how did you know where to find me? I didn't tell anyone where I was going. No one knew my plans."

"That's at least six, seven questions. I'm not in New York because, obviously, I need to be here. No, the litigation is not done and I'll be back in court on Monday morning. And as for finding you—well," he laughed briefly, "let's just say I have my ways."

She blinked a few more times. Shook her head. "I don't get it. What do you mean, you have your ways?"

He laughed. "I spent seven years in military intelligence. You didn't know that, did you?"

"Sam, I don't know a thing about you. Not since way back, you know, when we were in school." She sort of laughed. "If you can remember back that far."

"Oh, I remember, Marge. I remember everything."

She felt a pang. Embarrassment, definitely. It took some courage to keep from looking away from him. She kept her eyes on his face.

"That was then, Sam."

He didn't say anything for a moment.

"I hope that's true, Marge." He looked so serious, his usual, casual lightheartedness subdued. They both shut up for a moment, remembering.

Then Sam said, "Listen, are you feeling okay, now? Feeling steadier?" He looked over to where the crowd was thinning out. People were being loaded into police vans; reporters were shoving microphones into people's faces. "Let's get out of here," Sam said. "I haven't had breakfast yet. In fact, nothing since lunch yesterday. We worked late last night and I just had time to grab a candy bar at JFK before my flight. And then I slept through breakfast on the plane. You feel ready to go?"

"I'm okay," she said. She stood up—and wobbled a little.

"Here," he said. "Take my arm."

And she did, and she could feel the nice strength of him through the fabric of his shirt.

Oh, Lord, she thought. *He feels so good.*

Chapter Twelve

Coming out of the park, they were faced with a McDonald's across the street and a little further along, at the corner, a Pret a Manger.

"Oh, no," Sam said. "I didn't come all this way to eat at a fast food chain. Let's head back toward the hotel. I need to get a room and we can find some place to eat along the way." They started walking back along Bayswater Road, with the park to their left and on the right the long row of sedate homes and shops, all white and bright in the morning sunlight. Although there was so much to talk about, so many questions Marge wanted to ask, she was in a daze of confusion and delight that took her breath away, and silenced by a flood of emotions that belonged to another time.

She was glad she had his arm to hang onto. But the mystery of her attraction to Sam, so instantaneous and unexpected, silenced her, as well as the puzzle of Sam's gallant arrival, so impossible—so *magical*—so, for the time being, her questions remained unasked: Why was he in London? Why was he at her hotel? Why was he asking for her? How could he know where she was? She felt as though a door had opened and she'd stepped through into a fantasy place where impossible things happened. With her hand on his arm and his body so close against hers, she discovered that she'd have known this was Sam next to her even if she'd been blindfolded, even after all these years, as though the rhythm of his walk and the warmth if his body were an implanted part of her sense memory. How could that be? After twenty years? Impossible. Impossible, too, because of course his body was no longer the same. What had been the lanky, rather rangy awkwardness of his boyish, adolescent years had matured into a fit and fully adult male. She was intrigued by the transformation.

Sam Packard has grown into a pretty hunky guy!

She sneaked a sly glance at him, and realized it was true. She still wouldn't have called him hot-looking, not in a movie-star sort of way—but his hair was no longer wild, his expression was mature and more thoughtful, and though he wasn't handsome, he was definitely good-looking. And he hadn't lost that wonderful smile, a smile that said the world he looked out at looked good to him and that he was glad to be in it.

And so they walked for perhaps ten minutes, slowly, pleasantly, thoughtfully—and silently. Until Sam pointed to the left, where up ahead of them there was an entrance into the park.

"There's a cafe over there, in Kensington Gardens," he said. "I can get some breakfast." And as he led her across the street and through Marlborough Gate, he put his arm around her shoulders and pulled her to him. It was a gesture as friendly and familiar as though it hadn't been twenty years since they'd last been dating.

I'm too old to feel so young, she thought. *But oh, this is so sweet. So damned sweet!*

She leaned her head lightly against his shoulder, and she couldn't help closing her eyes in pleasure. He responded with a light squeeze of his arm around her and a light touch of his face against the top of her head.

Goofy! she thought. *I'm getting goofy again. That's what's happening. What am I going to do?*

At the cafe, there were empty tables outside in the sunlight, and he led her to one, pulled out a chair, and held it for her as she sat down.

"What would you like? They have sandwiches and salads and things. Tea? Coffee?"

"I've had breakfast. Just coffee."

"Do you still take it straight—black, no sugar?"

"Still the same," she said.

"I remember," he said. "You were just starting to drink coffee, and you thought it was very grown-up to take it black and straight. I thought it was cute." He laughed briefly. "I guess I was trying to be grown up, too. Feeling very superior."

"We were both doing our best," she said. "And now, look at us. We really are all grown up. Aren't we?"

"Right. All grown up." There was that nice smile again. "So, just coffee? No muffin? No scone? You're in London now. You're supposed to eat scones. Or a crumpet, or something."

Hadn't Dr. Diaz told her to gain back some of the weight she'd lost?

"Okay, a scone," she said.

"I'll get it," he said. He went to the counter, ordered eggs, sausage, hash browns for himself and coffee, black, for both of them. He brought a scone back to the table for Marge. Then they were ready to talk.

Marge started. "How long are you going to be here in London?"

"I have to leave tomorrow."

"Just the one day? That's a quick trip."

"Something I needed to take care of this weekend."

"Is it about the litigation? I think Jerry said one of the parties is a British investment house."

He didn't answer right away. He was choosing his words carefully.

"Sort of," he said finally. "I guess you could say it's connected with the litigation. Not about the Brits and their interest. No. It's something else." He put on a very serious face, and Marge had the feeling he was kidding. "You just never know where some big surprise will pop up."

"Sounds mysterious."

"Can't talk about it." Now he really smiled. "Confidentiality, you know."

"Well, okay. If you can't talk about it—"

"Exactly. So I'll change the subject." He tilted his head and looked her over, making a show of checking out what she was wearing. "I don't think I've ever seen you in jeans. That's a switch. Marge Webster, doyenne of the fashion industry, in jeans and a plain white tee shirt. Like an ordinary person." He leaned over to look under the table at her feet. "And tennis shoes," he added.

"Doyenne? That sounds so old."

"I don't know what else to call you. Anyway, what's up with the jeans?"

"I'm wearing a disguise."

He laughed. "Only you could make a disguise out of jeans and a tee shirt. But I get it. Now that you've become a celebrity—like if the tabloids knew—?"

She laughed at that. "I'm a very minor celebrity, Sam. But there are people who might recognize me if I walked around in my usual wardrobe, particularly around Mayfair. In jeans and tee shirt, I blend in very nicely. You're not going to give me away, are you?"

The waitress arrived with Sam's breakfast and he attacked his eggs. "Give you away?" he said lightly. "I would never give you away, Marge." Between mouthfuls, he added, "But it's a good thing I found you when I did."

"I know, Sam."

"I saw how that crowd had you trapped. It was getting pretty hairy."

"I was really scared."

"Of course you were. It was a really scary scene." He paused, his fork mid-way to his mouth, just long enough to check her out. "In fact, you're still a little pale." He smiled at her. "Eat your scone."

She took a bite. And put the scone back on her plate. "I'm not complaining about your being here."

"Good." He scarfed down some more eggs. "I'd hate to think I had to go rushing in like Sir Lancelot, at risk of life and limb, and have you be mad at me."

Oh, I'm not mad, Sam.

And then, Marge did a very uncharacteristic thing. Without thinking, without even noticing that she was doing it, she picked a hash brown off his plate and ate it.

But Sam noticed, and he smiled. He remembered that casually intimate act as one of her most endearing traits. He didn't know that she did it completely unconsciously, and that she had never done it with anyone else.

But when she licked the salt and grease off her fingers, Sam had to close his eyes for a moment, needing to control the response the innocent and unthinking gesture aroused in him. Momentarily more serious, he repeated, "Oh, Marge, a man would be a fool to give you away." Then, as though veering off in a completely different direction, he said, "So, Marge. Tell me about Jerry. How long have you and my worthy opponent been an item?"

"We've been together for about six years."

"Are you living together?"

"No." She knew she was feeling evasive. As though she needed to explain the relationship she had with Jerry. But why should she need to explain? And why be evasive? "We both have busy lives. We live independently. We're sort of—parallel. I guess that's a good word for it." It was the best she could come up with.

"Are you going to marry him?"

"Oh, come on, Sam. You can't just come waltzing onto the scene after all these years and start asking me personal questions."

"Fair enough. I'll back off."

"And what about you?" She gestured toward his left hand. "I don't see a ring. Any women in your life?"

She took another hash brown off his plate.

"There was. She was tall and dark, like you," he said. He didn't add: *but she wasn't you.* "We lived together for a few years, but she didn't like the military life and she didn't like Washington, DC. And maybe she didn't like me that much, either. Anyway, it didn't last."

"And nobody since then?"

"Nobody serious." She reached for another bit of his food and he laughed. "Listen," he said, "you must be hungrier than you think." He moved his plate over to her side of the table. "I've had enough and you can finish up what's left there. And then let's get out of here. I need to get back to the hotel and book a room."

She looked at the morsel of food she was holding. She actually hadn't realized it was there, hadn't realized she'd been picking food off Sam's plate.

"Oh, my God! I'm so sorry." She didn't know whether to eat it or return it to his plate.

"No. Go ahead. Eat it. Eat it all. I've had enough." He was laughing.

"That's so rude of me." She picked up her fork. "I didn't even realize—"

"I know. I think it's sweet. You don't remember, do you? You used to pick at my food all the time. Once, you picked the pickle out of my hamburger."

"I didn't!" And then it came back to her. "Oh, Sam. I did. I remember now. It was at a ball game. You set your burger down on the bleacher between us, and I didn't even think, and I just took it. And you teased me about it."

"Our team was winning and I was up on my feet, cheering them on, and when I looked around, there you were, eating the pickle out of my hamburger and not even noticing you were doing it."

"I was concentrating on the game."

"I know. It liked it, that you used to pick at my food."

"I don't know why I did."

"Doesn't matter. Anyway, eat up what's there now while I get the check. And we can go."

Chapter Thirteen

At the hotel, Marge waited discreetly in the lobby, curled up comfortably in one of the big tufted brown leather sofas. A copy of *UK Lady Fair* was on a side table and she leafed through it while she waited for Sam to book a room and leave a wake-up call for seven thirty.

He booked the room, but as it turned out, he never used it.

* * * *

He joined her at the sofa. "I'm set now." He sat down next to her. "And I'm hoping you didn't have any plans for the day."

"No plans. Usually, when I come to London, it's work, work, work. So I never get to just enjoy the city. This whole week, it's been really great. I've been just resting, walking around, people-watching. But you're here on legal business, aren't you? Don't you have to be somewhere? Or meet someone?"

"Not yet. I have some time. But as long as you're not busy, why don't we spend a little time together, maybe go people-watching together?"

"Okay. And while we're doing that, maybe you can explain how you just happened to be at my hotel. I mean, that is such a weird coincidence. I was so careful not to let anyone know where I'd be."

"Sure. I will, Marge. I promise. But later. Let's just enjoy this day first."

* * * *

In the years to come, Marge would remember that London was glorious that day. The skies were cloud-free and the city was bathed in sunshine. They walked along sedate streets that were lined with long rows of stucco-fronted houses gleaming white in the bright light, the air smelled clean as though newly rain-washed, and small neighborhood parks were lush with greenery that spilled out over iron fences. They walked for miles, and Sam's arm was around her shoulders, and they talked and talked and reminisced about the old days, the days when they didn't know they were still children, when their passions were roaring but not yet mature, when they resented the protections that surrounded them and kept them safe from their own wild yearnings. "Whatever happened to...?" they asked each other, and "Do you remember...?" recalling their favorite teachers and those they despised. They carefully did not mention that last encounter between them, the night of Sam's senior prom, the one that ended their relationship. They seemed, both of them, to know that they would have to save that for later.

So it was indeed a glorious day, and they spent it walking aimlessly, forgetting to get lunch and instead stopping occasionally for a coffee or an ice cream. They walked past Paddington Station and on up to Regent's Park, to the zoo, and visited the hippos and the gibbons. For a full half an hour, they goggled at the lemurs, who goggled right back at them. They had imaginary conversations with the gorillas and made up stories about the gorillas' inner primate lives and thoughts and conversations with each other. They left the zoo and walked down to Regent Street, and along the way, when Marge was attracted to the display in the window of a cute little boutique, Sam said, "Wait here a minute. I'll be right back." He ducked into a chemist's and was back right away with some items in a small plastic bag. "I needed a toothbrush," he said. "Have you room in your bag for this?" She could feel more than a toothbrush in the bag and gave a moment's thought to what he could have been buying in a chemist's shop—but then Sam reached into the bag and took out a packet of chewing gum, and she had to laugh at what she'd been imagining. "Some kind of British gum," he said. "It's called Air Waves. Want to try it?" She told him she hadn't chewed gum since she left high school, and he laughed and said, "Me neither, but I'm feeling like a kid today, so let's do it," and together they made a game of chomping their gum noisily. And then Marge saw someone she thought she knew coming out of the Kate Spade shop and she hid behind Sam while he shielded her behind a map he opened out wide, pretending to read it while they hustled back to Oxford Circus. It was almost evening by then and Marge's feet were killing her, so they got onto a bus, climbed up to the upper deck and from their lofty perch they looked down on passersby below and giggled like thoughtless adolescents, as though they were watching exotic and fascinating zoo-specimens, until they reached the hotel.

Up in her room, Sam called for a bucket and some Epsom salts. She collapsed into the room's one chair and Sam got down on one knee and unlaced her tennis shoes, resting first one, then her other foot, on his bent knee.

"You poor thing," he said. He removed her shoes and peeled off her socks. "I should have realized." Actually, he was laughing. "What a day you've had. Assaulted by a mob in the morning and made to walk miles all over London the rest of the day."

"You didn't make me. I had a wonderful time."

"You must be exhausted. Let's get room service to bring us dinner."

"Good idea. I couldn't walk another step."

There was a knock at the door and a maid arrived with the bucket and the Epsom salts. She glanced at Marge, sprawled on the chair, with her bare feet stretched out in front of her.

"Ah, there you go, luv." She gave each of them a big smile. "Happens all the time. Folks think they're good to go all day, and then they're not. Just give us a ring if you need anything else."

Sam thanked her, tipped her, and closed the door after her. Then he filled the bucket with really hot water, stirred in the salts, and set it at Marge's feet. He rolled up her jeans and she put her feet into the hot water.

"Oh, God, that feels so good."

He picked up the phone to call room service.

"What should I order for you?"

"A hamburger of course. If they have it. With tomato and a pickle." They both laughed. "And fries. Or 'chips.' Or whatever they call them here. As long as they're French fries."

Sam called and made sure his order was understood, and he added a bottle of red wine to the order. When the food arrived, there wasn't any place in the tiny room to put the tray, so Sam told the young man to put it on the bed. After he left, Sam fixed Marge's burger for her, spooning ketchup out of a little serving dish, and laying the pickle over that. He put her plate on her lap, and then he fixed his own hamburger. He opened the wine, filled their glasses, and put hers on the small table between her chair and the bed. Then he got himself comfortable on the floor next to her feet, with his back against the bed and his plate and glass on the floor next to him.

"Okay, Sam," she said as she picked a couple of fries off her plate. "I can't wait any longer. I've been patient till now. So, are we ready to really talk now? Obviously, the legal business that brought you to London couldn't have been very important, because you haven't done a thing about it all day. Either that, or that isn't the reason you're here. So, what is it?"

Sam shook his head and laughed. "Oh, Marge. I can't talk seriously with a girl whose feet are sore and who's got them soaking in a bucket of water." She started to protest, but he held up a hand. "No. No. Let's have our dinner first, and drink some wine, and maybe get just a little bit buzzed, so we're all happy. Then, when you're properly dried off and your feet aren't hurting any more, we can talk."

"You promise?"

"I promise."

His expression had become so gentle and so serious, she couldn't help herself. Without thinking, and just as naturally as she might have brushed a wisp of her own hair away from her face, Marge put out her hand and brushed back a bit of Sam's hair that had fallen over his forehead. And she saw that he closed his eyes ever so briefly at her touch, as a cat might do, being petted.

"Oh, Sam," she said. "You didn't come here on business, did you? You came here to see me."

"We'll talk about it later, Marge. Eat your dinner. Drink your wine."

"But you'll tell me, won't you? How did you know to come to London? I didn't tell anyone where I was going? And how did you know where I was staying?"

"Later, Marge. Later."

So they ate their hamburgers and drank their wine, and turned on the TV to catch ten minutes of the latest news which didn't match their happy mood so they turned it off and promised themselves no talk about the outside world. And then, when they were the tiniest bit tipsy from the wine, Sam got a towel and dried off Marge's feet. He put the tray of dishes on the floor outside in the hall, to be picked up by the maid. Marge, still barefoot, got up onto the bed and sat cross-legged at its head with her back against the headboard. She scooted over to make enough room so Sam could sit on the edge of the bed, facing her.

"Okay," Marge said. "Now it's time to talk."

"All right, Marge, first of all, how did I find you?" He laughed. "Actually, it wasn't all that difficult. There was your Instagram post from the airport. Actually, I can show you."

"From that post? You can't. There's no way—"

"Well, there are ways. True, it's a little sneaky. But you know what they say. 'All's fair in—'" He paused, looking a bit sheepish. "Well, you know what they say. Anyway," he pulled his phone out of his pocket. "Here, I'll show you."

And there it was, her Instagram post from the night she left for London. Sent from the airport, while she waited at the gate, getting ready to board, and the text:

> *Tally ho! going off the grid—into the wild blue—don't look*
> *for me for a few weeks—or months?*
>
> *I'll be in touch when I get back to New York."*

And pics of her shoes, a glass of wine, the book she planned to read.

"Look there," Sam said, pointing. You can see in the background, the information board at the gate. It's a little indistinct, but I was able to enhance it. Shows your flight's departure time, the destination—London—and the flight number. Also, the British Airways logo. So I knew where you were headed. Also, the 'Tally ho!' was kind of a giveaway—fox hunting and all that."

Marge stared at him. And at the picture on his phone. And back again to Sam. She didn't know whether to laugh or cry.

"But isn't that illegal—or something—?"

"Well, not exactly illegal. Not nice, I admit that. Not something I'd ordinarily do. But Marge, aren't you glad I'm here? And weren't you glad this morning, when I was there to pull you out of that crowd at Hyde Park?"

She was still befuddled.

"But even if you knew I was in London, how did you know—"

"Which hotel? Well, that was a little more dicey." He paused, choosing his words. "Yeah, I crossed the line a little on that one. You know how, here in England, you have to hand over your passport when you check into a hotel? And they're required to record all the information from it? Well, I contacted an old buddy in British army intelligence and asked him to do me a solid. He had a friend at the Foreign Office who owed him a favor and, well, I guess my buddy sort of owed me one. So my buddy's friend did a cross-check of the hotel passport registrations, and that's how they found you here. Now we're all even—me, my buddy and his friend. Bending the rules, I guess, but —"

"Bending? It sounds to me more like breaking."

"Well, maybe, Marge. Just a little. But it's done and here I am. And anyway—not really broken. These guys deal in life and death stuff all the time. This was just a happy little favor they could do for an old friend and in a good cause. And no harm done."

"So you went to all that trouble, calling in old favors, maybe 'just sort of' breaking the law a little, and flying overnight, transatlantic, just to spend a day with me here in London? What for?"

His response didn't come easily and while he thought about how to answer her, she took the time to study his face. She could see the boy she'd once thought of as "older" still in there, still animating his expression, still giving it the happy, light touch she remembered from when he was, really, just a boy. But what she also saw—or perhaps what she could only glimpse—were the twenty years that lay between then and now. Now there were those twenty years and the man he'd grown into, the man who'd moved on beyond his boyhood, who'd had a love and lost it, a man who'd dealt with serious issues, probably "life and death" as he'd suggested. She could only guess at what was left of the kid he'd once been. His answer now might tell her a lot.

"What for?" He repeated her question. "Why did I come?" After a long, thoughtful pause, he said, "That's the hard part to explain. But I'll try." Again, there was a long pause, as though he'd rehearsed this part and wanted to be sure he got it right.

"Every now and then," he began, "I see your name and your picture in the papers or on TV. I know you're being successful and you're doing exactly what you'd always said you wanted to do, and I've tried to be happy for you. I believed the door between us was permanently closed and that what was in the past was definitely altogether in the past. I've tried not to think of what I felt for you way back then, tried to think we've both moved on with our lives." He stopped, took a deep breath, and forged on. "And then, there I was that evening, it was only a couple of weeks ago, coming out into the corridor from the courtroom, and my mind was full of international banking regulations, and strategizing the case and planning to meet with my team, and a brief the judge had just asked for—and there you were, sitting on that bench out in the corridor, and I swear, Marge, I was gobsmacked, all over again. Just like when I was a kid. Everything fell out of my head and all I could think was, 'There she is. That's my girl!'"

Her face registered her protest, but he stopped her before she could say anything.

"Of course, you're not really my girl. I know that. You're someone else's girl. And I realized that right away. Not only someone else's, but the guy who's sitting at counsel's table on the other side. So I said to myself, 'Okay, Sam. Back off. Don't make a fool of yourself.' I don't poach another man's girl, Marge. I figured I'd just have to be a grown-up and accept that you—and I—and our lives, too—have moved on, and what's in the past has to stay in the past.

"But it was making me crazy, sitting in that courtroom every day, watching Jerry Germaine doing his job against me, and thinking how he must be going home to you every night, and that he was the luckiest guy in the world. It took everything I had to keep my mind on the case. And then I ran into the two of you at the Brahma House that night, and I had a chance to watch the two of you together. What I saw told me you're not really his girl. Not really. And now, today, you've told me, you've been together for six years and you're not even living together. What was it you said this morning—you're 'parallel'? Yes, that's a good word for it. That's what I saw. Two lives sort of running along together, but not bound, not bonded to each other. And after that night, when I saw that, all I could think was I had to connect with you, find you, talk to you, let you know that I'm here and that I want to open that door that we closed that night, twenty years ago. I couldn't wait. It was getting into my head, every day, every hour. I can't work like that. I can't live like that."

"So you decided to come over, spend the day with me. And then? What did you think would happen then? Tonight?"

She studied his face and saw that he understood her.

"Marge, I didn't come here to take you to bed. Though God knows, even now, sitting here on this bed, I feel like I'm eighteen years old again when I was a kid and I wanted you so badly it was painful, when all I could think was I had to sleep with you or I'd bust."

"But you can't—"

And here, Sam took both her hands between his, and held them to his lips and kissed them gently. And his eyes, which had never left hers, seemed almost to plead with her.

"I know I can't. Even if you were willing, there's no way I'd be able to sit in that courtroom for the next weeks, with Jerry Germaine on the other side, and know that behind his back—you and I—"

"And this is okay? Your being here with me? Even if it's just to talk? Just to walk around the streets of London? Just to spend the day together? Just to sit together in this tiny room, with both of us up here on my bed? That's not behind Jerry's back?"

"I know. But I couldn't stand it. I had to find out how it is between you two. I have to know—are you—in love with him? Is it a lifelong thing?" He rushed on, not giving her a chance to answer. "It's just—I never forgot how it ended between us, and I've been so sorry. A thousand times, I blamed myself, like I was older and should have known better. But Marge—you're not fourteen anymore, you're a grown-up woman. And you're different now. You were sort of a wild one back then"—she began to protest and he laughed and made a gesture to stop her—"a nice wild one, believe me, and you were fun. I don't see that same 'fun' now. Now you're all adult and serious and a hot-shot big executive. If that's how it is—okay—it's not my business. But if it's Jerry, if he's not fun with you, if you don't have that wild spark anymore because of him, or if you truly want to be only the hard-driving person I see in the papers and on TV, the big executive powerhouse you are now and nothing more, well, okay. But I had to know."

He took a big breath after all that.

"And that's why I'm here," he said. "And if you wanted to, I would sleep with you tonight. No, I'd sleep with you this minute." He stopped, and Marge saw his hunger for her, and she felt her own hunger for him surge through her. "But it would be a bad idea," Sam said, "and I can't speak for you, but I'd be sorry later on."

She put her hand on his arm and she saw him flinch. She knew he was right, they'd both be so sorry later on. And they were, both of them, grown-ups. So she did nothing more than let her hand rest on his arm, and she nodded, agreeing with him.

"So that's it," he said. "I've declared myself. You know why I'm here. And now I'd better go." He laughed. "Before I forget all my noble words and my damned code of honor."

Marge laughed, too. "Oh, you were always such a Boy Scout, Sam. But you're right. You have to go," she said. "You have to get out of here. Right now. I mean it Sam. Go now. Leave now and go back to New York."

"I will. I'll head out to Heathrow now. I can catch a plane out tonight." Her hand remained on his arm and they both knew she didn't want him to leave.

"Go," she whispered.

He didn't move. "Will you let me kiss you goodbye?"

She couldn't answer—torn between a loyalty to Jerry, her sense of honor, and by her desire for Sam—he was so close, she couldn't help herself, the smallest nod of her head—

And Sam had his answer. He made no move to take her in his arms, but he bent his head toward her.

This was no eighteen-year-old's kiss. This was a long, slow kiss that made a promise even as it said goodbye.

She pressed her hand against his chest.

"Go, Sam. Go now. Go quickly."

He understood. And he left. And she stared at the door after he closed it behind him, and her heart was beating, so hard—so hard.

Chapter Fourteen

She didn't sleep well that night. How could she? She'd taken Sam's kiss to bed with her and it remained with her, for better and for worse, through the hours till dawn brightened the curtains at the window. The "better" part felt like a gift, a sweet present wrapped up in tissue and ribbons and scented with the rarest of perfumes. That's the part that should have lulled her into sweet dreams.

But the "worse" was the wagging finger of accusation, scolding her for cheating on Jerry.

But it's not cheating she argued back at her conscience. *Jerry and I aren't exclusive. We never agreed to be exclusive. Not that there's ever been anyone else. But still—*

And for goodness' sake, it was just a kiss!

Oh, but what a kiss that had been. Magical. Mystical. Mysterious. All that, and more. She had to admit to what her conscience already knew: if Sam had chosen to stay, she'd not have been able—no, would not have *wanted* to stop him.

Well, her conscience put it to her, *isn't that the same as cheating? Even if you didn't do the actual deed?*

And so she struggled, back and forth all night, only occasionally dozing off fitfully and waking again from confused dreams and uneasy rest. Altogether, she slept hardly a full hour through the night.

* * * *

At dawn, she gave up the effort, showered, dressed and went out into a lovely Sunday morning. She paid no attention to where her feet were taking her, hoping the early-morning quiet of the empty streets would soothe the conflict that had kept her awake through the night. But instead, the mental battle she'd created seemed to have developed an almost physical reality. She imagined Sam and Jerry walking right along with her, keeping her company, glaring across her at each other.

Stop it! she told herself. *Pay attention to where you're going, what you're doing. This isn't good for you. Dr. Diaz wanted you to rest, avoid stress, get yourself calmed down. At this rate, you'll be a nervous wreck by the time you have to get back to work.*

But still, her imaginary companions demanded her attention. Without realizing it, she was retracing her path from the day before, and wherever she went, she kept up a silent conversation with the two men: with Jerry, she was pointing out the sights, as though she was now an experienced guide and he was a tourist—and with Sam, she unconsciously rewound the tape of the day, re-experiencing his voice, his touch, and the feel of his presence. At Marble Arch, for Jerry's benefit, she described the crowd and their near-riot, the arrival of the police, the reporters and news trucks, and the gaping onlookers. But to Sam, she replayed her panic, the feel of his hand on her arm when he pulled her away, cleared a space for her, made her safe. To him she expressed again her gratitude, and her astonishment at the fact that he was there at all, but to Jerry, she said only that it was a pretty hairy scene. When she came out of Hyde Park and thought to get a coffee at the McDonalds across the street, she "told" Jerry, *oh, no, there's a much nicer place further down, at the cafe near the Italian Gardens, inside the park, in Kensington Gardens.* But it was her hand on Sam's arm that she felt as she walked along Bayswater Road, and though she "showed" Jerry the gate where they could enter Kensington Gardens to get to the cafe, it was Sam's arm that went around her shoulders again. When she ordered breakfast at the cafe, she asked for eggs, sausage and hash brown potatoes. To Jerry, who knew she usually had nothing more than coffee and maybe toast or a plain bagel for breakfast, she said that the London air must be making her unusually hungry, but to Sam, she smiled slyly and said, *now I won't steal yours.*

It was a very schizophrenic experience, and it persisted all day. After breakfast, she circled back up and around Cleveland Square, walked way past Paddington Station and on up to Regent's Park. Along the way, she pointed out to Jerry a large ice cream parlor, glass-fronted and bright, beginning to be busy this bright Sunday morning and told him that there was a super variety of flavors available here in London, at the same time that she smiled, and in memory again shared with Sam a heaping cone of peanut butter and salted caramel ice cream. At the zoo in Regent's Park, she again visited the gorillas, where she introduced Jerry to Kumbuka and Mjukuu and their two babies and imagined mama Mjukuu asking her *where's the cute guy who was here with you yesterday?* And explaining he'd had to go back to America. From the zoo, she walked all the way down past Oxford Circus, along Regent Street, paused for a long time at Hamleys—five floors of toys!—asked Jerry if he thought a Hamleys would do well in New York now that FAO Schwarz was gone, but her question to Sam was about having children, did he want kids, how many, would he care if he never had children?

* * * *

By the time she got back to the hotel, her feet were killing her again, and again she needed a bucket and some Epsom salts. And once again, the maid commiserated. But this time, there was no one to take off her shoes and massage her feet. She wondered if Jerry would think to do that. He would do it, she was sure—if she asked him. Probably. Unless he only laughed. But Jerry never seemed to think she needed any help or pampering of any kind. This was the price she paid for being so independent and competent! She tried to imagine Jerry kneeling at her feet, rolling up her jeans.

While she soaked in the Epsom salts, she thought about how she and Jerry met.

Six years ago. She'd been getting close to thirty and one of the editors at *Lady Fair* decided to play matchmaker. "Boy, do I have a man for you," the colleague had said. "Good-looking, smart, up-and-coming young partner at his law firm, unattached—" It was to be nothing more than a date, but they met, they laughed together, he called her again, they got along really well, and somehow they drifted into a regular thing. Yet she'd never agreed to marry him. Why had she never said yes? He was good to her. They got along so well. There'd never been an angry word between them. Maybe—some day—maybe sometime in the future, if she were to decide that she wanted children. But in the meantime, her career had taken off big-time, she was at the top of her profession, and she couldn't see anything beyond *Lady Fair* and the powerful presence she currently occupied in the fashion industry. Hadn't that been her dream forever? Distractions were not wanted, not while things were going along nicely.

And now?

And now, there was that kiss.

But if Sam's appearance now wasn't a distraction—for heaven's sake, what else could it be? Could she possibly think of him in any way except as a hiccup in her very grown-up life? A passing fling. A momentary flash of adolescence. A mysterious bit of recovered memory.

And so she went—back and forth.

Did she owe Jerry an explanation? Was she willing to explain? *Could* she explain? Would he understand? Did she even, herself, understand what was happening? Six years with Jerry were not, God knows, to be treated lightly.

But never, not even in the early days, the courting days, of their relationship, had he ever kissed her the way Sam did. Last night.

She ordered in a dinner, took a soothing bath, and went early to bed, determined, this night, to sleep well. And she did sleep, but tonight her dreams were filled with zoo animals, especially the big daddy gorilla and his mate and their babies, and they were all wagging their fingers at her, and laughing.

Chapter Fifteen

She woke up laughing, too. "Okay," she said aloud. "I've had it with all of you! You can just stop bugging me." She got out of bed and went into the bathroom.

While she brushed her teeth, she told the mirror, "I'm supposed to rest and recuperate. I'm supposed to avoid stress." In the shower, she closed her eyes and held her face to the stream of water. "For one week, I'm not going to think of either of them. 'No' to Jerry. 'No' to Sam. They can battle it out in court. And I can't let them make me crazy."

She knew this was a promise to herself she wasn't going to be able to keep—not entirely. But she could make a serious effort, for the sake of her mental health. And her physical well-being. That one near-fainting episode had scared her and she knew she needed to take better care of herself.

She dressed and went downstairs to the dining room to have her breakfast there. No more retracing steps. As she ordered coffee and a bowl of berries and yogurt she wondered, momentarily, how Penny was doing. And Bridey's next piece for her column. *I liked that street food idea. We could do something nice out of that.* Then put those thoughts out of her head. Nothing work-related allowed! She was determined to think only simple thoughts, solve no problems, and avoid fashion, *Lady Fair*, and most of all, men. She would not even read the newspapers. The world could spin along without her observations for a while. At least for a week. Then she'd reevaluate. She'd already turned her phone off, and on the way out, she gave a lavish tip to Mr. Marley, the hotel's concierge, and told him to contact Jerry and her office and inform them from her that if they really, *really* needed to reach her, he was the person to call and he would forward any messages to her.

She kept her promise to herself, at least mostly. She couldn't help it that Sam and Jerry intruded, but when they did, she'd think of Kumbuka laughing at her and wagging his finger, and then she'd laugh, too, and shut the door on them.

They both know I'm not supposed to be bothered. So they'd better leave me alone!

In the days that followed, she sat in the park and read her book, she rode buses around town to enjoy the city, impressed as always that it was a totally up-to-the-minute place, built up over a very ancient footprint. She avoided the zoo, which was now full of memories—and those teasing gorillas—and she just let the days wash over her. She spent one day riding out to Stonehenge, and walked solemnly around that remarkable place, thankful that it had been kept as desolate as it should be, five thousand years old; it deserved to be preserved with respect. Back in London, she went to a couple of movies, bought a theater ticket for one evening. On Saturday afternoon got herself lost in a tangle of streets and alleys around Middle and Inner Temples until she finally tumbled out onto Fleet Street where, just beyond the end of Chancery Lane she stopped, intrigued by a shop that made barristers' wigs, robes, and other paraphernalia. Despite her promise to think no fashion thoughts, she couldn't resist and she spent a fascinated hour interviewing the salesperson, learning the arcana of the making and wearing of lawyers' and judges' wigs. She considered buying a wig as a souvenir to take home to Jerry, but they were expensive and what in the world would he do with it? So she just thanked the clerk for his time and attention and left the shop and continued her wandering.

Just beyond the Law Courts, she passed a travel agency. On a whim, she went in, leafed through several brochures, and with no forethought at all, she booked a flight, leaving on Monday, for Vienna. She'd never been to Austria and didn't know anyone there. She chose it out of the blue. It would be her next getaway stop where she'd surely be anonymous and could explore a city whose only meaning to her was waltzes and whipped cream. Oh, yes, and the horses. The famous white Lipizzaner horses. The agent booked a room for her in an obscure *pension* near the center of town. She stuck the tickets into her bag and went out into the afternoon sun, feeling like a happy thief in the night, making a great escape.

She considered taking a ride on the Eye, but she knew the giant Ferris wheel would be jammed with kids and weekend tourists, so she let that idea go, thinking she'd save that for her next trip to London. And the new zip line was too terrifying even to consider trying that. So the rest of this day would be just for lazy wandering around. In her bag, along with the airline ticket to Vienna and the room reservation, she also had a ticket for the Guy Fawkes celebration that evening at Cleveland Square. That sweet Mr. Marley at the hotel had advised her not to miss the fireworks and bonfire display and had seen to it that a ticket was waiting for her at the desk when she came down to the lobby that morning. There'd be a barbecue at the celebration and drinks—mulled wine, beer, soft drinks—so she didn't stop for dinner, and just needed to be sure to be there by six when the gates to the private park would be opened to ticket holders.

The November days were becoming chillier, so she stopped at her hotel room and picked up a sweater, then went on to Cleveland Square. People were already milling about when she arrived, holding their drinks and plates of food and chatting each other up, and someone put a glass in her hand and gave her a plate of beans and ribs. It was much like Halloween, with children running around in Guy Fawkes masks and a sense of deliberate mischief in the air. By the time the traditional bonfire was ablaze, Marge was feeling a little bit prosecco-buzzed and she wondered if she'd made a mistake, deciding to leave London and go on to Vienna. With only one day left, she was now feeling very affectionate toward this city that had been her home for these last two weeks; the anonymity it had allowed her had been a new and delightful experience. But she also wished she could be experiencing this party with a friend. With Bridey? With Bridey and Mack? That would be fun. To share this noisy, giddy, fire-filled, uproar of a celebration, one piece of England's so-often violent history.

And then, in a rush, her imaginary conversations with Sam and Jerry returned.

I wish you were here with me.

But who was she talking to? She had no idea. It was as though her wish went out into the London night, willing either one of them to be there at her side.

Maybe I'm not used to being at a party where I don't know anyone, where no one knows me, or even knows who I am.

But that's what I wanted, isn't it? To be unknown for a few weeks?

She went back to the buffet table and put some more baked beans on her plate along with another couple of ribs. She was surprised that the menu included such typically American barbecue fare. She had her glass filled again—more prosecco. And by seven fifteen, when the fireworks began, she was eating ribs and feeling nostalgic and happy and lonely, all at the same time.

Her gaze was skyward, the night was filled with corkscrew flares and shooting lights and noise and rock music and the scatter of screaming, excited kids and all the ooh and aahs that go with a fireworks display.

And through the racket, a quiet voice next to her said, "Some display, isn't it, Marge?"

She closed her eyes.

Sam?

She turned, and there he was, smiling at her. It was as though she'd wished him there, out of thin air. As though she'd conjured him out of the fireworks. Into the midst of this crowd.

And this time, he didn't ask for permission. He took the glass out of her hand, and right in the middle of all those people, all those strangers, in the dark and lit by fire and shooting stars, he put his arms around her and he kissed her, fully, thoroughly, and with great authority.

Then he smiled, licked his lips, and said, "Mmm. Barbecue. Delicious."

She was staring at him. Her heart was going so fast, and she couldn't breathe. He pulled her close and laughed. He had to shout over the noise of the fireworks.

"Yes, it's really me. I tried to stay away. But I couldn't. I just couldn't." Then he kissed her again, lightly this time, and said, "You'd better breathe. You look so spooked."

She managed to inhale slowly, and then she gasped.

"I'm not supposed to get stressed."

He gave her glass back to her. "I can't hear you," he shouted. "Here, you better drink this."

"What the hell are you doing here?" She barely got the words out.

"I can't hear you." Still shouting.

She tried to shout at him. "What are you doing here?"

He shouted back at her. "You know what I'm doing here. I couldn't leave it where we were last week."

"What?"

"I've had a rotten week. It's been hell."

"I can't hear you!"

He made a face up at the shooting lights. "Let's get out of here. I can't hear anything."

He took the plate and glass from her, put them on a nearby table, and took her hand to lead her through the crowd, and out to the street, where it was a tiny bit quieter.

"Where are we going?" she said.

"Where do you think? We're going back to the hotel." He was still holding her hand.

In the circumstance, she couldn't think of a good alternative. She was so stunned, she wasn't able to put up an argument. And as they left the square, and walked farther away from the noise of the celebration, they could hear each other more easily.

"Sam, I don't understand. How did you know where to find me?"

"That nice guy at the desk, Mr. Marley. He knew where you'd be. You might want to have a talk with him. He seemed to *want* me to find you."

"But you'd have needed a ticket to get into the park."

"That was Marley again. Very resourceful guy. Like any good concierge, I guess. It's almost like he was expecting me."

"Oh, Sam. I don't know what to say. You shouldn't be here."

"Are you sorry?" He stopped her, right there on the street. He turned her to face him. The light from the fireworks still shooting up in the sky played across his face. "If you really don't want me to be here—" He hesitated, as though it was hard to say it. Then he continued, "If you mean it, I'll go."

She didn't dare say what was in her heart and she let him read it in her eyes.

And Sam understood, and he took her in his arms and his kiss was full of fire and fireworks and music and it was magical, all over again.

"I want you to stay," she whispered "I do want you here, Sam. I've tried all week to not think about you, and now you're here, and I do want you to be here. But—" She looked into his eyes, hoped he could see into her heart. "But you shouldn't. We shouldn't—" She was shaking her head. "You know it isn't right."

He was holding her close to him and she could feel his heartbeat matching her own.

"We can't talk here," he said, "in the midst of all this racket. The whole city is partying. Let's go back to your hotel. It'll be quiet there, and we can talk."

Chapter Sixteen

She should have said no. She knew that. She knew that you can't take two fully adult, grown-up people, each desperately hungry for the other, and put them into a hotel room together, and not know that they're going to wind up in bed. The truth was, she felt so excited that Sam was there with her, his arms around her had felt so wonderful, it was impossible for her to push him away. So, as they walked back through the streets of celebrants, with the giddy noise and the flare of fireworks all around them, the raucous party-goers and masked children running about, waving Guy Fawkes effigies, and the feeling that the whole city was having a good time, Marge knew what she was asking for.

But at the hotel, she made a last effort to resist the inevitable; she insisted that he book a room for himself. And she insisted that they sit in the lobby to talk.

"I can't stop you from staying here," she said, "and I don't know what you were expecting, but I can't let you spend the night with me."

"What I was expecting? I had no idea what I was expecting, except to come back to London, to spend a few more hours with you. To spend the night with you, if you'd let me." He saw the expression on her face. "Yeah. To sleep with you, if you'd let me. If you're willing."

"And Jerry?"

"Well, yeah. Jerry Germaine is the problem. We've been in court together, every day, looking across counsels' tables at each other, watching each other across the courtroom, fighting it out really hard on both sides. But I have an unfair advantage, because I know what he doesn't know, that it's not just about our clients and their interests. Because my 'worthy opponent' doesn't know that I've been here with you, seeing the city, walking around, having fun. That I'm here again now, hoping for more than a kiss. Behind his back. It's unfair—I know, that's what it is. It doesn't matter what they say, about all's fair in love and war. This feels so wrong—I can't tell you how wrong it feels. And still, here I am, Marge. Here I am, so crazy to see you, to hold you, to take you to bed—I'm behaving like a maniac, flying transatlantic, just to be with you for a few hours. For the night, if you'll let me."

She struggled, trying to sort out what it was she was supposed to say to him. The same old arguments—*Jerry and I never promised anything—we never said we'd be exclusive—after all, am I not free to be attracted to anyone?—and Sam and I go back a long way—and I feel so good with him, so young and silly—it feels so sweet—*

And while she struggled, while Sam waited for her to figure out what she needed to say to him, the hotel's doors burst open and a noisy group of revelers spilled from the street into the lobby, bringing the party inside with them. They swirled around, filling the grand old space, laughing, tumbling about, splashing their drinks.

Sam smiled at her. "This conversation is too serious to be out in public," he said. "Let's continue it upstairs in your room where it'll be quiet. I promise I won't even touch you, if you don't want me to." As they passed the desk, he said, "Wait a minute." He wanted to have a bottle of wine sent up. Marge waited while he did that.

What are you doing, Marge? she said to herself.

She knew perfectly well what she was doing. She was letting her resistance to temptation slip away.

As they walked up the broad, marble staircase, she knew that all her internal, mental arguments had only one purpose. She was trying to justify letting Sam be with her.

I shouldn't. I know I shouldn't. It's not fair to Jerry. I know.

But we never promised each other—

How would she be able to tell him?

She wouldn't need to tell him. He needn't ever know. But how ugly that would be between him and Sam. If he found out.

I shouldn't.

I can't help it.

Chapter Seventeen

She opened the door. The room was dark, and only the city's light at the window, only the flare of fireworks everywhere let them see each other. With a single motion, he closed the door behind them, had his arms around her, and was kissing her.

"We shouldn't—" she tried to say it.

"I know. Oh, God! I know!"

He was kissing her again and they were both on the bed.

"I'll be sorry," she whispered, letting him kiss her again and again, returning his kisses.

"Me, too," he said.

The light sweater she'd picked up earlier that evening was already off and tossed to one side. He was pulling fiercely at his tie, trying to tear it off, and she was clutching at the buttons of his shirt. It seemed that clothing was there just to drive them both crazy.

Her tee shirt was off. His belt was unbuckled.

And still they were kissing, unable to let each other go. The bonfires and the fireworks were forgotten. The rules and the city and the room around them—all forgotten.

Deaf to the world.

Deaf to the world—almost.

But the ring of the telephone broke through.

He was unhooking her bra. She was peeling his shirt off him.

And the phone was ringing.

"Leave it!" he gasped.

"I can't."

"Leave it! Let it ring!"

She heard his urgency. But a thousand things raced through her head.

"I can't. I left only an emergency number." She felt like sobbing. She was staring at the phone.

Sam also turned to look at the phone, which continued to ring. If looks could kill, that phone would have melted away right there on the end table.

Sam took his hands off her. She let him go and he stood up. "Okay," he said. "I'll get it." He picked up the receiver. He barked at it. "Yes?"

Marge sat up, staring at him while she re-hooked her bra. Who could be calling? Who was in trouble? Who needed her?

But Sam's face registered no emergency. He looked at Marge, and he shook his head slightly, reassuring her. No emergency. And then, whatever it was, he apparently thought it was funny. Sort of.

"Sir," the voice on the phone said. "It's room service, sir. You ordered a bottle of red wine?"

"Yes."

"Well, I'm sorry to disturb you, sir, but we didn't know if you wanted it delivered to your room, sir, or"—the man hesitated—"or perhaps you'd prefer to have it delivered to the lady's room?"

Sam's expression was not hard to understand. Irritated, mostly. Frustrated. But also amused. He smiled at Marge and his smile said it all. He shook his head.

"Well, room service, you found me, didn't you?" he said. "Bring the wine here, to the lady's room. And bring a couple of glasses, too."

Marge took a deep breath. She understood.

Sam hung up the phone. Marge was getting up off the bed.

"Oh, no," he said. "Don't go." His arms were around her.

She laughed and pushed him away gently. "We both knew we shouldn't. I'm taking it as a sign from heaven."

"You don't believe that."

"Doesn't matter. That's my story and I'm sticking to it."

"You're going to drive me nuts, Marge."

"Nonsense." She was getting off the bed. "You're the sanest person I ever knew. It'll take more than a little frustration to drive you nuts."

He turned toward her as she went toward the bathroom. "I'm not as young as I used to be." As she closed the door, he called after her, "It's not a little frustration. This sort of thing isn't good for my heart."

"Your heart is just fine," she called back.

He started to pick up the scattered clothes. "Next time, I'll disconnect the phone first."

"There won't be a next time." He could hear the water running.

"Yes. I'll be back. You'll see."

"You won't find me. I'll be gone. I'm leaving London on Monday."

"Where will you be?"

"Not telling."

"I'll find you." He picked her bag off the floor where she'd dropped it. It had fallen a little bit open. He glanced inside and saw what was there. "Where are you going?"

"Really. I mean it. You won't find me."

With practiced fingers, he opened the bag a little wider, just far enough. The plane ticket was teal blue, with the logo, the long red bird shape, over the letters "AUA." He smiled to himself. Austrian Airlines.

"Oh, yes I will," he called to her. "I'll find you." The other paper was the receipt for her reservation at the *Pension Kreindl.* On the *Kumpfgasse* in Vienna. "You can't hide from me," he said. He smiled, closed the bag and put it with her clothes on the bed. She came out of the bathroom, brushing her hair, and he kissed her, gently.

"That was pretty intense," she said. "I'm glad the phone stopped us."

Sam sat on the edge of the bed and pulled her down next to him. They sat there together, like old friends.

"It wasn't the phone," he said. "It was you. You stopped us."

"Whatever. I'm glad. I felt like I was cheating. I've never cheated on Jerry. I'd have been so sorry, later on."

"You're probably right. At least, I'll be able to face him a little more easily in court."

"How's the case going?"

"It's a tough one. And your guy is very good."

"How long, do you think?"

"Probably about another two or three weeks."

They both sat silently, thinking. Minutes passed.

Marge spoke first. "Why is it, do you think, that a kiss, no matter how passionate it is, isn't as bad, as wrong, as 'the deed' itself?"

"I don't know. But you're right. We sort of allow lusting, but draw the line at actual fornication."

They both laughed at the old-fashioned word. "Seems to me," she said, "they ought to be equally wrong, but it doesn't feel that way."

There was a knock at the door, and Sam said, "Enough of the morality check. That'll be the wine."

"Thank God!" They said it together.

* * * *

"This is feeling kind of homey," Sam said, "this room. Feels like a replay of last week."

They were sitting together on the bed, side by side, feet on the floor, drinking their wine. Marge just nodded. She was feeling it, too.

"Did you know?" she said. "You left your toothbrush here. It's in the bathroom, in the water cup. Along with mine."

"Yeah. I knew I left it. I liked the idea of its being here with you, sort of intimate, and ready for me to come back." He put an arm around her and put a light kiss on her cheek. "So here we are. Like we're a comfy old married couple. With my toothbrush next to yours in the bathroom, and the British telly we can watch till we fall asleep."

"You're not going to sleep here. You have your own room. You can go watch television there."

"Yeah, I know. But we can drink our wine and talk for a while. Then you can send me to my room."

"It's not a punishment."

He laughed. "I know. I'm just kidding. I'm kind of jet-lagged anyway. And I'll bet my room is at least a little bigger and more comfortable than this one." He looked around him and his gesture took in the cramped space, the pictures that decorated the very limited wall space, nondescript landscapes and fox hunting scenes, and the single window looking out over a very sedate row of white stucco-fronted houses. "How come you picked this hotel, of all places? So small and so out-of-the-way? And such a small room? You live a pretty lavish life back home. I'd have expected you'd be in a big suite, with all the amenities and the upscale service. You could have stayed at the Ritz, or one of those big hotels over by the Palace."

"This place and this room, they're exactly what I wanted. Small and unobtrusive, and no likelihood I'll run into anyone I know here." She looked around. "This little room is sort of my bat cave. It's what I needed. For rest and recuperation."

"You've really worn yourself out, haven't you?"

"I guess."

"And now you need to get back to a sane and safe place. Back to who you once were?"

"That's about it. And guess what?" She smiled at him. "Like magic. Here you are. Someone who knew me when I was—the person I used to be."

"I'm not just someone, Marge. I'm the guy who remembers how you were."

"Who knew me way back when."

"Right. Back when you were an eccentric teenager who dressed outrageous and had big grown-up dreams and the talent and drive to go with them, and was already on her way along the path that was to take her to—"

"To—?"

"To where you are now. Editor in chief of *Lady Fair*, industry powerhouse, recognizable wherever she goes—"

"And under doctor's orders to take a break—or break down." She laughed.

"Yes, Marge. That's right."

They were both silent for a long time.

And then Marge said, "So what went wrong between us, Sam?"

He didn't answer her right away. Finally, he said, "We were both incredibly young."

"I know."

"You never answered my letters."

"I know."

"I wrote to say I was sorry."

"Oh, Sam. You always were a decent guy."

"Did you even read my letters?"

"No. I threw them away."

"That's too bad. They were beautiful letters. I worked very hard on them." He laughed.

She laughed, too. "I'll bet."

"I have a confession to make."

"Oh?"

"That first day, Marge. In the cafeteria at school? When I came over to ask the girls about their plans for the future?"

"I remember."

"I'd created that whole story about an article for the school paper, just to have an excuse to talk to you. I'd already seen you around school and I wanted to meet you."

"You'd noticed me?"

He laughed. "I could hardly help noticing you. You were very noticeable."

"I guess I was. I wanted to be."

"And when I saw that seat next to you, saw that it was empty, I saw my chance."

"Why do kids need to be so devious—instead of just walking up and saying, 'I'd like to talk to you'?"

"I know. Always so scared of getting it wrong."

"And I remember, when you sat down—" She paused, then turned to look directly at him. Her eyes questioning his.

"Yes," he said. "I remember. We just barely touched, and it felt like something happened between us—something passed between us—something special."

"Yes—"

"I always wanted to ask if you felt it, too. But I was afraid."

"So was I."

"There *was* something special between us."

"Yes. There was. Back then."

"We should have been more careful. That night. After the prom."

"I know."

"We were awfully young, Marge."

"I know. Awfully young, and much too proud."

"I've replayed that night a thousand times in my head."

"So have I."

"I shouldn't have said what I did—about your future, not taking it seriously enough. I just couldn't imagine a little girl from a small upstate town, getting to run the premier fashion magazine in the world. Seemed so unlikely to me. I thought I was being mature and realistic. You were right to get mad."

"I was awfully hurt. I'd started the night feeling so grown-up, so—so *validated* by your interest in me. And then you were shooting me down. Telling me to be—oh, I don't know—just ordinary! I thought you knew me better than that."

"I should have."

"Well, I've worked very hard to prove myself. To be not ordinary." She laughed. "And look where I am now. On the verge of a nervous breakdown!"

"And hiding out in a bat cave in a foreign land."

"London doesn't feel like a foreign land."

"That's true."

"And I'm glad you found me, Sam."

He said nothing for a long time. Just gazed at her. And then he nodded, as though he'd just had a long talk with himself.

"I'd better get out of here now," he said. They both stood up. "But I'll see you in the morning. Before I leave. There's something I want to show you."

"Something to show me?"

"In the morning," he said. At the door, he pulled her close. "I'm sorry you're wearing yourself out," he said. And his arms were around her as though to make a protective barrier against the whole world, and his kiss was the kiss that had begun with a magic touch between them so long ago.

Chapter Eighteen

She was barely awake when Sam arrived at her door.

"I need my toothbrush," he said.

She laughed and gestured toward the bathroom. And got back into bed.

"I wasn't ready to get up yet," she said.

"I'll give you ten minutes." He went into the bathroom and came out moments later, brushing his teeth. Through a mouth full of toothpaste, he said, "I've got a plane to catch later this morning."

"Mmm."

"Ten minutes!"

She disappeared under the covers and he went back into the bathroom, rinsed, and came back out. He had a newspaper with him, and he sat down in the one chair and opened the paper.

"Ten minutes," he repeated.

No answer, and he smiled toward the bed and then began to read.

Ten minutes later, he looked at his watch, folded up the paper, and went over to the bed. Her hair was a mass of dark curls on the pillow, and he lifted them so that he could lean down and put a kiss on her cheek.

"Time to wake up, sleepyhead."

"Mmm."

He pulled the covers back a bit, exposing her shoulder. He shook her lightly. "Come on," he said. "Gotta get going. Get up. Get dressed. Come on," he repeated. "I'll buy you breakfast."

She opened an eye. "Where are we going?"

"You'll see."

Tabloid articles and profile pieces about Marge Webster described how she had her hair and makeup done professionally every morning, and how her wardrobe was put together very carefully for each day's scheduled activities. Well more than an hour could be spent just getting her ready to leave for the office.

So Sam was impressed to see that she also knew how to be ready—bed to front door—in ten minutes. Jeans, tee shirt, a denim jacket and Top-Siders. Hair pulled up into a ponytail. And her handbag slung over her shoulder.

"Where are we going?"

"Into the park. Into Kensington Gardens. Something there I want to show you."

"Can we get breakfast first? Coffee, at least?"

"Sure. What I want to show you—it isn't going anywhere."

* * * *

The colors were changing in Kensington Gardens; the morning was autumn-cool and Marge was glad she'd brought a jacket. But the tables were still outside at the cafe near the Italian Gardens and as they took their seats, she liked that the same table they'd sat at the last time was free; she liked to think of it as "our place." Sam went to the counter to order their "usual" breakfast of sausage, eggs, and hash browns, came back to the table and then sat back in his chair and said, "Listen, Marge. There's something I have to talk to you about."

"You look serious. Is it serious?"

"I'm not sure. You'll let me know."

"Okay."

"After I left you last night, I was thinking."

"Yes?"

"Well, you were saying you're leaving London tomorrow. And you wouldn't tell me where you were going. And I said I'd find you, and I was kind of teasing about it."

"What are you getting at, Sam?"

"Well, I guess I thought it was kind of a game. Like you could pretend to hide and I could pretend to hunt for you. And it was fun. We were sort of teasing each other."

"Yes?"

"But when I was back in my room, thinking about it, I realized this trip away from New York has really been a kind of retreat—you really do need to get away from everyone and everything. And I've been so eager to see you, it never occurred to me that maybe I'm getting in the way of your recovery."

"Hardly that, Sam."

"I'm glad to hear it. But twice now, I've just shown up, unannounced, unplanned for, never asked if it was okay with you."

"It's been okay. It definitely has been okay. Surely you could tell. I practically ripped your clothes off you last night."

He laughed. "Yeah. Well that was encouraging, it's true. But here's the thing. Last night, our things got kind of scattered around on the floor, and while you were out of the room, when I was picking up our stuff, your bag was open and I saw your plane tickets."

She opened her mouth, but no words came out. She couldn't decide if it was funny, or outrageous, or just what she wanted, and before she could choose a response, he went on.

"And your room reservation."

She was even more—what?—confused?

"Yeah, I know," he said. He understood. "Not nice. But I thought it was kind of cute. Here you were saying you wouldn't tell where you were going, and I was saying I'd find you. And I was thinking I knew how to find you and I would just arrive and surprise you in Vienna. Like we were playing a game.

"But then it occurred to me, 'Sam, you're practically stalking her. That's bad. Maybe Marge really does want to be left alone. Maybe she really does *need* to be left alone. Maybe, if you get together in Vienna, it should be only if that's what Marge wants.'

"So I want to suggest this, Marge. I expect we'll be in court this week at least and maybe the next couple of weeks. If you decide you want me to come over, just text me and the first day we're free, I'll be on a plane that night, meet you anywhere. But if I don't hear from you, then I'll know to just look forward to when you're home, all rested up and recuperated, and we'll see what's what at that time. How does that sound?"

By the time he'd finished his speech, she'd closed her mouth. Now she just stared at him for a while. She blinked a few times, as though to clear her head. And finally she found her voice and she said, "Sam, you're too much. Here I was thinking it *was* kind of a game. You were saying you could find me and I was wondering if you really could—I was even kind of hoping you could. But I also really do need to rest and be lazy for a few weeks, and walking around foreign cities is good for me. I'm a city girl and I don't need nature to restore my soul. I just need to be away from work. In Vienna, I can sit in a coffee house and drink one of the local brews—I hear they have more variations than Starbucks—and I can read my book, and not need to be anywhere, nor need to think about anything.

I can take a walk in the Vienna Woods. I can watch those white horses. The Lipizzans. See their show. I hear you can watch their training sessions. Maybe I'll do that."

"It was thoughtless of me. And selfish."

"I don't want you to think that. Not at all."

"I just wanted so much to see you."

"Yeah, and I was thinking you must have really been some sort of spy because you said you worked in intelligence. I hoped you really could figure out how to find me. That was kind of romantic, the notion that maybe you were a spy—like maybe you were CIA."

"My lips are sealed about that." He laughed.

She laughed, too. *"Vee haff vays to make you talk."* she said.

"I'll bet you do."

And right at that moment their breakfasts arrived. Sam waited till the cute waitress got all the plates settled in front of them, and left. "So, do we have a plan?" he asked.

Marge cut her sausage and speared a piece with her fork. "I'll have to think about it."

Sam loaded up his fork with scrambled eggs. "I won't bug you about it. Not another word." He looked around, and up at the sky. "We can talk about the weather."

"It's a great day," she said. "Good flying weather."

"Getting a bit nippy."

"It's fall."

"Right."

Then they both laughed.

"So," she said. "You wanted to show me something this morning. Before you leave."

"You'll see. It's not such a big deal. Except to me. Eat up, and then we can go."

She knew he was eager to get to it, whatever it was, so she didn't ask for a second cup of coffee. As soon as she'd finished her first, Sam got the check and paid it.

"Ready?" he said.

"Ready. Let's go."

They walked back toward the Lancaster Gate and then walked down the path that went past the Italian water gardens on their left. To their right, great swaths of lawn were beginning to lose their summer green, and all along the way the trees were turning autumn-colored, foliage that grew thicker as the path continued past the Long Water, where the path was bowered by trees that were all sunlit orange and russet and gold. He drew her hand through his arm. "Isn't this park the greatest?" he said. "Whenever I'm in London, I try to find time to get over here for a visit. Especially right here, this path. This is where we're headed." A little farther on, the trees thinned and there was an open area to their right. Beyond a low iron railing that ran about a hundred feet or so, there was a clear space, and at its center, up a couple of low steps of round concrete platform, there was a statue. It was about fourteen, maybe fifteen feet tall, and there was the figure of a boy at its top, a boy astride the twisty, thick mass of small bronze figures below.

Sam led her through the gate and up to the platform.

"This is it," he said. "This is what I want to show you."

"This statue?"

"Yes," he said, pointing up at the figure of the child. "See? It's Peter Pan. Playing his pipe, up there on top of that pile of fairies and swirls and tangles of—I don't know—trees, I guess, and caves and little animals, rabbits and mice and squirrels. Little woodland things. It's been there for over a hundred years. Barrie himself helped create it and had it secretly installed overnight without any permission from anyone. As a surprise for London kids."

Marge walked up to it and touched the cool metal. The little figures that made up the massive base, which was maybe ten feet tall, were so intricately entwined, it was difficult at first to make them out, but the little boy up at the top, his figure was very clear. A slim, life-size child, a boy of perhaps eight years, in a kind of short, fluttery night-shirt, astride the pedestal of fairies and little creatures, one arm outstretched to his right, the other holding out the long pipe he was playing; yes, of course she recognized him. This was Peter Pan, the boy who never grew up.

She studied the figure for a minute and then turned to look at Sam, who was studying her studying the boy. His face was lit up with pleasure at the sight.

"I didn't know you were a Peter Pan fan," she said.

"Oh, yeah. I really love this kid."

"Because he never grew up?"

"That's it."

"And that's what you wanted to show me?"

"That's part of it." He looked around, as though he wanted to be sure they were alone. "I'm going to tell you something I've never told anyone. And I'm going to show you something I bet no one else has ever seen."

"I'm intrigued."

He hesitated, as though to encourage himself to continue. And then he did.

"When I was a kid, I came here to London with my folks. Dad had business here and he decided to make a vacation of it and brought the whole family. Mom and me and my kid sisters. And one day, it was my twelfth birthday, and we'd had a sort of little party at a restaurant nearby, and then we all came here to see these gardens. And there was this guy with us, a business acquaintance of my dad's, and he had given me a birthday gift, a book. It was called *The Little White Bird*, and it was written by J. M. Barrie and in it Barrie had included an earlier version of his Peter Pan story. In that story—it's only a part of the bigger story, a few chapters—Peter is only a week old and stays only a week old forever and it takes place almost entirely here in Kensington Gardens around places any London kid who played in this park would have known. Like a New York kid would know the Alice in Wonderland statue in Central Park. Or the Sheep Meadow. Or the zoo.

"So, this friend of my dad said I should know that story, too, because it's the original Peter Pan story and it's different from the one most people know, and in a way it's kind of sad. And because we were in the park anyway, he thought we should see this statue, so we came over here.

"Well, there was something about its being my birthday, and turning twelve, and feeling like I was going be all grown up—going to *have* to be all grown up—that made me look at this kid—" Sam gestured up at the bronze boy. "And I felt like I had to make some kind of permanent connection with him. Something that would keep the 'boy' part of me forever, no matter how much the rest of me grew up." Sam paused, and he looked at Marge with an expression that seemed mischievous and sly and sad and cautious all at the same time. "You won't tell anyone, will you?"

"I promise." She wondered what she was getting herself into. But repeated it. "I promise. I won't tell anyone."

"Well, my dad had given me a Swiss Army knife for my birthday, and I had it in my pocket. And when they all went down the path, to watch the swans on the Serpentine, I stayed behind and I took that knife and—" he took her hand and led her around to the side of the statue, "—and here, I'll show you." He paused behind a spot about half-way up the base, under and just a bit behind Peter's outstretched right arm. "Here." He pointed to two bronze fairies, almost hidden in the swirls of the massive dark form. They seemed to be in a close embrace, the one turned forward but with her face turned back over her shoulder toward the other who, behind her, clasped her tightly, their bodies wrapped sensually together. They were about to kiss, the two heads close to each other, cheek against cheek.

"Don't tell me—" Marge was surprised. Not at all something she'd have expected of Sam Packard, a congenitally good, honorable, law-abiding guy.

"Yes. I used that knife, and here," he pointed to a spot, in a shadow just below a swirl of the fairy's robe, she could see the tiny letters scratched into the bronze: "S.P." For Sam Packard.

Marge was just shaking her head, her eyes fixed on his. She was speechless.

"Yes," he said. "I did that." He didn't look at all remorseful. "I made this statue mine," he said. "And whenever I'm in London, I come here and check it out. I make sure no one's discovered it and had it polished out."

"You're not sorry, are you." It was a statement, not a question. Was she disapproving? Maybe a bit, and maybe not.

"Not exactly—though, in a way, I am. Of course. Because I grew up. I learned not to do things like that." A little sheepishly, he corrected himself. "No, even then, I knew I shouldn't do it." Then he shrugged. And laughed. "But there it is—my crime, etched in bronze. Leave it to me, if I'm going to commit a crime, I do it so it would be easy to catch me, and pin it on me. The evidence would last forever. Still, I know that practically every kid has some sort of little crime in their past. Shoplifting a candy bar. Spray painting someone's garage door."

"That's true," Marge said. "I once took a little bracelet of carved red beads because the color exactly matched the blouse I wearing. And I didn't need to steal it. I had money. It just felt like an irresistible wickedness. Like something I *had* to do. I honestly felt that bracelet *belonged* to me and it had no business being displayed on a counter in a girls' clothing store in a shopping mall. "

"How old were you?"

"Eight." She looked at that "S.P." on the statue, and rubbed her thumb over it. "I still feel ashamed about that bracelet."

"Well, that's the thing. I never really felt ashamed about this." He pointed to the scratches. "It was like I really needed to make a permanent declaration, somehow. That no matter how grown up I'd get to be, it was absolutely, vitally important that I not lose *all* of being a kid. Like it was a necessary part of being a real man, whatever that is. Maybe a way of saying no matter how much grown-up responsibility I'd be willing to take on, some piece of me would remain irresponsible. The piece of me that would need always to be taken care of. The piece of me that would never be able to grow up. Sometimes I think that's a way of being able to be loved." He stopped. He was thinking over what he'd just said, realizing it sounded pretty murky. Then he added, "I don't know. Maybe that's why Barrie needed to have Wendy in the story. And Mrs. Darling."

"Something to think about," Marge said.

"Yeah. I guess. But here's the thing, Marge. The reason I wanted you to come here with me, to see this statue—not just to see what I'd done to it. Not just to confess my crime to you. My little crime. I wanted you to think about your own growing up. And about keeping something for yourself that's *not* grown up. That will never be grown up."

And here, Sam took Marge's face in both his hands, gently, as though they held a delicate flower, and lifted her head so that he could look deeply into her eyes. "Marge, my darling. I knew you when you were young. When we both were young. And you were a like a—oh, I don't know—like a bubbling mountain stream, with the light dancing off you, all sparkly and flowing and full of changing colors. And I look for that girl now inside the strong, big-shot corporate executive you've become. Is she still inside there, inside the woman who runs a really huge enterprise, who hires and fires people, who's so driven and so hard-working that she's on the verge of collapse?"

Neither one of them spoke for a very long minute.

And then Sam wrapped his arms around her and held her very close and with his face close to hers, he said quietly, "And I saw you that night with Jerry and I saw no sign of that bubbly, sparkly girl. I saw nothing that told me that this was anything but a relationship of social convenience, two nice people who get along well enough, but neither of whom excites any passion in the other. A nice, business-like relationship. Efficient. Adequate. Maybe even long-lasting. Marge, darling, it breaks my heart."

She could feel his heart beating against her chest, and knew that he must feel hers.

"Sam," she whispered, "that night—the night of the prom—I'm so sorry. That shouldn't have happened."

"I know."

"We shouldn't have let it happen."

"I know.

"But that was so long ago. And no matter what you say, I'm not that girl any more. And Jerry has been an important part of my life. Six years now."

"I know."

"I'm not making any impulsive decisions."

"Of course not." They both smiled. This was the grown-up, mature, adult Marge Webster talking.

"And you have a plane to catch."

"Right. And you'll be on your way to Vienna tomorrow, and God knows where you'll be after that."

"Right. And maybe I won't want you to join me. So that I can have a chance to think with a clear head, without your charms to distract me."

Sam laughed. "My charms?"

She slapped playfully at his shoulder.

"Let me go," she said. "You know how charming you can be."

"Okay." He looked at his watch. "And you're right. I do have a plane to catch. But first, there is something I want to give you."

"Oh, Sam. A gift for me?"

"Yes. A gift." Again, he held her face in his hands, and this time he was looking at her mouth, as though making a decision. "A charm." And then he tipped his head very carefully, as though he needed to find the exactly correct place, and very, *very* lightly, he put a kiss just at the corner of her mouth. It was a kiss so gentle, it was barely more than a breath of air at her lips. She felt the tip of his tongue touch that tiny spot, right there, in the corner of her mouth.

"There," he said. His smile beamed at her. "That kiss belongs to me. I've never given it to anyone else. And no one else can take it from you. I buried it as deep as I could. So now it's ours." He laughed broadly, because she was staring at him, as though she'd never seen him before. "What?" he said. "I mean, kissing you is nice, but I didn't expect to knock you speechless."

How could she tell him? A warmth had spread from that spot through her whole body, right down to her toe tips and up to the edges of her ears. For a moment, she hadn't been able to breathe, and she thought she was again about to faint. She was trying to recover her voice, trying to return to a normal conversation.

Sam was unaware. He had his arm around her shoulder and they started up the path past the Long Water, walking toward Bayswater Road.

"Anyway," he was saying, "wherever these next weeks take you, I hope you're going to decide to let me join you. I don't want you to be hiding from me."

She had taken a couple of deep breaths and recovered her voice enough to say, "We'll see." Then, as they approached Lancaster Gate and Sam hailed a taxi, Marge was able to laugh and say, "I hope you have a really hard time facing Jerry in court this week. You should have guilt written all over your face."

"No way," he said. "In court, I'm a shark. Remorseless. No mercy. No conscience. Peter Pan could be ruthless, you know."

Marge laughed. "That's true. And you lawyers, too! A pox on all of you!"

And then, when the car arrived and he was about to get into it, he turned to kiss her goodbye. This was not a passionate kiss. Just a plain, old-friends, goodbye kiss. Because he could be seeing her soon in Vienna. And because she was carrying that kiss hiding in the corner of her mouth that belonged to him.

"Oh, shoot," she said. "I still have your toothbrush."

"That's okay." He got into the car, closed the door, and through the open window, he said, "Hang onto it. You never know. And while you're in Vienna, have your first breakfast at Demel's, on the Kohlmarkt. And think of me."

He waved goodbye, and she called after him.

"Safe trip."

Chapter Nineteen

Marge thought a couple of hours up in the air at thirty-six thousand feet would get her away from the turmoil of Jerry versus Sam. She was wrong. The two men might as well have been actually sitting there, one on each side of her, crammed into her not-so-comfortable coach seat on the way to Vienna. How was a girl supposed to rest and recuperate while her fantasies were preoccupied with the two men, each of them poking at her like a nagging kid, wanting her attention? She couldn't seem to turn them off. Sam was so appealing. But so was Jerry.

She needed to shut them both up and just get on with her plan to do nothing but take care of herself. She hoped Vienna would be a good place for that. She knew no one there, and she knew very little about the city. Of course, "Vienna" meant Mozart and Strauss waltzes and whipped cream. She knew that much. And the beautiful blue Danube. All that sounded restful.

Maybe I can dump the two of them into the river!

But when her taxi from the airport wound its way through the tangled streets behind St. Stephen's Cathedral and pulled up in front of the *Pension Kreindl*, she realized she was still imagining that she was sharing the event with her fantasy Jerry and her fantasy Sam, with each of them in turn, and the internal conversations continued:

Marge: *Look. Look at that. Look, Sam, look at the cobblestoned street. Must be centuries old.*

Sam: *I'm glad you wore casual clothes for the flight. A girl in Jimmy Choos could kill herself on those stones.*

And then to Jerry.

Marge: *Have you ever seen anything like it? A whole city of baroque architecture.*

Jerry: *I know. It's like a Disney theme park. I should have brought a good camera with me.*

The street was so narrow, there was just room to open the taxi door and shoehorn herself out of the taxi and into the *pension*. She entered through a door topped by wrought iron filigree and flanked by elaborately draped and half-naked stone caryatids, and found herself inside a very small lobby with a desk and a smiling concierge who took her passport, confirmed her reservation and handed her the key to her room, two flights up. There was no elevator but there was an attractive winding staircase with a banister—also of beautifully decorative wrought iron. The room was small and not elaborate, but there was a vanity table with a tall mirror, the chair and the dresser were Biedermeier, and she had a strong sense that she'd been dropped into a time long past. Perfect for forgetting everything. She was now ready to get rid of her two annoying, imaginary companions. She told them most forcefully to shut up and leave her alone, and each of them slunk off into their imaginary corners, pouting. She deposited her carry-on, washed up, slipped a guide book into her handbag, and went downstairs to ask about breakfast.

But she was too late. The little dining room was already closed and breakfast was no longer being served. The concierge gave her a map of the inner city, wrote down a few suggestions, and Marge left the *pension*.

The day was lovely, crisp and November cool, and people moved briskly along the twisty streets, many of which were so narrow, she marveled that automobiles could squeeze through. She wandered without a plan, enjoying the freedom of being unmoored from everything—from work, from responsibilities, and mostly from being a grown-up woman who'd spent the last couple of weeks flitting around in a fantasy-like teen-aged romp with a man who had disappeared out of her life twenty years ago, and who maybe should have stayed there. And who presented the question: is that what she wanted?

Don't think about that! Not now! Not today.

She wandered past the Stephansdom, crossed the Stephansplatz, went down a narrow street she recognized from an old Orson Welles film and turned into the Kohlmarkt which, from her map, she knew was where she'd find Demel's. She knew she could get a late breakfast there, because even she, who did not know the city, knew of Demel's which was about three hundred years old and was famous for its pastries. *Lady Fair* had once featured a story about the place and she was eager to see if it was as fabulous as the writer claimed.

There were tables set up outside on the narrow sidewalk, but all were taken, and in any case, she preferred to see the interior. Which turned out to be indeed fabulous, with gleamingly polished dark woods and chandeliers of great globe clusters and high coffered ceilings and many tall display cases along the walls. But all that was nothing compared to the glass-shelved *étageres*, all bearing pastries and candies, rows and rows of them, and counters and serving tables covered with platters of cold meats and small sandwiches, bowls of pasta salads and vegetable salads, everything exquisitely prepared and presented, the array and the variety overwhelmingly beautiful and seductive.

There were several rooms, mirrored and gleaming and not crowded, and she took a seat at one of the small round marble tables near the front window. She remembered the description of the waitress's uniforms from the magazine's article and she smiled to see how accurate it was: designed hundreds of years earlier, a kind of loose smock of a soft glazed fabric, black, belted, longish and very plain.

She ordered the asparagus tips in tartelettes and the cold stuffed veal in aspic and, while she ate her late breakfast—or was it her early lunch?—she looked around to study her neighbors. Difficult for her to tell but she thought they were a mix of tourists and Viennese, the latter being one elderly gentleman in a sedate dark suit who was reading his newspaper and having a mocha, ladies who'd been out shopping and were now meeting for a coffee and, at the table nearest her, a woman who was surely well into her eighties or more, quite tiny and fragile looking but elegantly dressed in a long gray woolen tunic over a short skirt. She was perfectly groomed and was wearing some very correct and very serious jewelry. The others seemed to be an assortment of American and German and Italian and Polish visitors who were obviously examining every detail of the decor and the service and the ambiance.

The old woman at the next table was looking at her check and opening her handbag to take out her wallet. Marge sized up the outfit in order to identify the designer but then quickly corrected herself. *That woman has a dressmaker.* She glanced discreetly at the woman's shoes and to herself she added, *and those shoes are handmade.*

Their eyes met ever so briefly, the tiniest of smiles passed between them, and Marge went back to trying to decide on a pastry for dessert.

She chose the hazelnut-and-chocolate cake and from the great variety of coffees on the menu, selected a *mélange.* She took her guide book from her bag, opened it up and thought to begin a plan for the day while she waited for her order to be brought to her, when the woman at the next table, having paid her bill, got up and to Marge's surprise stopped beside her.

"I don't wish to disturb you," she said, "but do you mind if I ask, you are American, are you not?"

She spoke excellent English but with a slight Viennese accent and a charmingly gentle and well-bred lilt. Marge liked this woman instantly.

"I don't mind at all," she said. "Yes, I am American. Why do you ask?"

"May I sit down?"

"Of course." Marge was charmed by everything about her. Her gracious manners, her excellent clothes, her lovely voice. She moved with a bird-like delicacy and with minimum fuss. Her hands rested in her lap. She sat very erect.

"I have been coming here to Demel's since I was a child—oh, it's been so many years now. It was always such a lovely place, and to be brought here by my grandmother for a treat, to be allowed an ice cream or a chocolate. And this was my grandfather's *Stammcafé* after he retired. Every morning, he'd arrive at ten, sit at his usual table—this same table where I now sit—and have his usual newspaper brought to him, drink his customary *melange.* And precisely at eleven-thirty, pay his bill and leave. The same, exactly, every day.

"In those days—that was before the war—here at Demel's, they were such grand people, in their beautiful clothes and the visitors from other countries, I loved to hear all the foreign languages. It was like being taken to a show in a theater. But in those days, it was expensive to travel, so the visitors from other countries, tourists who came into Demel's, they were perhaps people making the grand tour, or Czech aristocrats on their way to their summer place in Crimea, or Germans on their way to the Swiss ski slopes or American physicians wanting to meet Dr, Freud. But later— you know, after the war—when things began to return to normal"—she paused, but only briefly— "after the war, we had the occupation and only Americans had the money to travel, at least for the first years. And then the students began to arrive, and there were business people expanding their interests into Europe. Oh, it became all quite different then.

"And so, after the war, when I came into Demel's, when I was grown and could come to Demel's without my grandmother, there were so many new people to watch. And I made a game of trying to guess where they were from, just by looking at their clothes, their shoes, seeing what they ordered, how long they stayed. I do so enjoy what one calls people-watching.

"And when you came in—into *Demel's*—in jeans! And a tee shirt. I thought *she can only be an American.* But Americans order only coffee and a piece of cake, and they leave quickly. So then I thought, no, maybe she's Swedish. The Scandinavians are always on a hike, or some sort of wilderness excursion."

Marge smiled. She was enjoying this woman still more. She'd had no idea she'd been under observation.

"And what did you see? Beside the jeans and the tee shirt?" she asked.

"Two things. First, when you sat down, you looked at the chair, quickly. Your hand lingered momentarily on the distinctive top. You noticed the design—I'm sure you realized that the decor is in the Biedermeier style of the eighteen hundreds—and I saw the very tiniest smile, as though you approved. The leather cushions are, of course, a commercial addition, suitable for a restaurant. And then you ordered the asparagus and the veal. Not customary choices for Americans visitors. They seem to prefer the sweets. And then you ordered the nut cake and the *mélange*. Not typical. Usually the Americans order the Sachertorte. They've heard of it and then they are disappointed to discover it is quite a dry cake. They don't know it's supposed to be, for a reason."

"I hope you'll tell me."

The woman laughed. "Ah, I've talked too long already. I'd hoped only to chat with you just a tiny bit."

"But how did you decide, with all that, that I am an American?"

"It was the mix of things. The casual clothes. The self-confidence. You are here alone, without companion, and not shy. The sophisticated sensitivities. Also, what we call"—and here she lifted her hand and touched her thumb-tip to the other finger-tips—"we call it *fingerspitzengefühl*—a sensitivity, as though in the fingertips. Also, I must confess, there was one other thing."

Marge laughed. "Perhaps you saw my passport."

The woman laughed, too. "No, of course not. It's your face. Despite the jeans and the tee shirt, I've seen your face somewhere. I'm quite sure of it. I can't place it, but it will come to me. You are perhaps a famous movie star?" But then she drew back a bit, quickly. "Ah, but I see that does not please you."

It was true, of course. And for a very brief moment, Marge's face said so, but she quickly made light of the idea. She laughed. "No. Heavens, no. I am most certainly not a movie star. And I can't imagine where you might have seen my face. I've never been to Vienna before."

"Ah, then I have been wrong. But not about the 'American' part. You are an American, and you have been kind to let me sit with you for a moment." She stood up. "I will leave you to your guide book. And I hope you enjoy your stay in Vienna. But before I go," she opened her handbag and took out her card case, "I will give you my card. While you are visiting here in Vienna, if you need some assistance or would like just to have a coffee, you may call me." She took a small, gold pen from her bag. "I will write my telephone number." In the lower left corner, she wrote the number and handed her the card.

Marge read the name, engraved in conventional italic font on heavy card stock.

Christiane Riemer

Only the name. Nothing more. Marge thought fondly of her own grandmother, who also carried a card case with her calling cards printed with only her name engraved on them. Marge had not seen one like this in many years.

Marge watched Christiane Riemer disappear through the door and out onto the street. Looked again at the card. And put it into her pocket. She turned, momentarily, to her fantasy Sam and said, *I've just met a delightful Viennese lady—*

And then remembered that she was *not* going to be drawn into any more imaginary conversations with him. Or with Jerry. She banished them again to silence and focused on her guide book.

* * * *

She let her feet take her where they chose, with no guidance from her and she found herself at the top of a long flight of stairs, perhaps a hundred steps, leading down toward the Danube Canal. At the bottom was a quiet space with a small, plain church tucked away amid the surrounding buildings. Her guide book told her this was the Ruprechtskirche, Vienna's oldest church, by legend founded in A.D. 740. She decided to go inside and had to smile as she crossed the quiet plaza toward the entrance. A timeless scene was being quietly enacted in the shadows outside the church. Off to the side, at the edge of the little plaza, there was a bench. And on the bench there was a couple, a young man and a young woman, and they were locked in a long, long kiss that Marge had observed as she had been descending the many steps from the Morzinplatz above. They made no move, even as she passed by them to enter the church, oblivious to all, aware only of each other, and Marge felt such a tenderness toward them, it almost brought tears to her eyes. Oh, to be so young. And to be so public with one's love. And to have so little sense of the complexities that lay ahead.

She sighed, feeling old and wise, almost as though she were as old as Christiane Riemer, and then she went into the cool, spare interior of the church, where she spent an educational half hour or so, enjoying its very simple Romanesque grace and beauty. Her guidebook told her everything she wanted to know, perhaps somewhat more than that, and she was ready to leave to walk farther on down, to the Canal. She wondered, as she left, if the kissing couple would still be there on the bench when she came out onto the plaza and laughed to herself to think that if they were, that would indeed be a kiss for the record books.

But no, they were gone and the bench was empty. She decided to take their place and sit for a while on their bench to have a think before she continued her walk.

I miss Sam. It would be fun to have him here with me. That young couple would have given him a chuckle, so innocent they were.

And I miss Jerry, too. He'd find all this so interesting. He'd have spent a couple of hours inside the church. He'd have devoured all the information from the guide book and the printed materials they had available.

What am I going to do about those two?

Chapter Twenty

After a few more days of wandering aimlessly about the city, through the ancient, winding streets inside the Ringstrasse, after sitting for comfortable hours in the Stadtpark or near the Gloriette behind Schönbrunn Palace, reading or doing a bit of fashion sketching, just for fun, after a full morning at the Prater where she had a lunch of wurst and beer and treated herself to some of the rides, including the giant Ferris wheel, the Riesenrad, which she also recognized from the same old Orson Welles movie, she realized she was beginning to be tired of all the rest she was getting. She had to laugh. Tired of resting! Tired of being unproductive, unbusy. She was feeling much better, more like her old self, more like the woman who could cruise through days of effort with no feeling of strain. If it weren't for the dilemma Sam Packard had brought into her life, she was ready to believe she hadn't a care in the world. Damn Sam! Why did she have to feel so young and happy when she was with him? Why did he have to show up at all?

Why did he have to have gone to law school and become a really good lawyer—as good as Jerry—and of all things, so good he wound up on the other side of a case against Jerry? Why had fate arranged things so that she went to the courthouse that day? If she hadn't, he'd never have seen her there. If all that hadn't happened, she wouldn't now be trying to sort out all this confusion, which heaven knows, she didn't need in her busy life.

So maybe, instead of going home to New York at the end of the week, she'd stay on in Europe for another little while, and let the whole problem simmer a couple of weeks longer—and see if she decided to write to Sam—or not!

She'd been thinking of contacting Christiane Riemer, and was feeling ready to make a little human contact. Lunch perhaps? Or a mid-morning coffee?

She got Christiane's card out of her wallet and first thing the next morning, dialed her number. She'd already dialed when she realized it was early—perhaps too early—but Christiane sounded wide awake and said she was delighted that Marge had called. "I think we quite liked each other," she said, "and I am free this morning. Shall we meet at the Cafe Sacher, let us say in half an hour? It becomes so crowded later, but we should be able to have a table if we are there before ten."

And so they were to meet. Marge decided jeans and a tee shirt would not be the appropriate attire for this meeting and was glad she had packed one pair of proper dark trousers and a creamy cashmere sweater from The Row—just the thing as the days were cool—and a pair of Prada flats, sturdier than ballets but not quite sneakers, good for extended walking around town. When she arrived at the Cafe Sacher, she was led to a table where Christiane was already waiting.

"If you were Viennese," Christiane said, laughing, "I might have come a bit later. It is our custom to be just a little late. But as you are American, I was careful to be here on time. Americans are always so punctual."

"We are?" Marge was surprised. "I never thought about it." She, too, laughed. "How late is proper?"

"Fifteen minutes. It is our Viennese *viertel*—a quarter of an hour—our permission to be a bit lazy. A custom that is dying out, I think, as we become more efficient and modern."

"It sounds like a good idea. Sometimes, we Americans work so terribly hard, we wear ourselves out."

Christiane said nothing, only lifted her head a bit to signal the waiter who arrived instantly. She ordered a kipferl and coffee and Marge said she'd have the same, and when it came, she discovered that a kipferl was an incredibly delicious, buttery croissant, bent into a full crescent, a little sweeter and a little smaller than the stateside version. Christiane gave her a brief history of the croissant which was in fact an import from Austria by the French at the time of Marie Antoinette's arrival from Vienna to make her doomed marriage to the young French king. Its crescent shape was created, Christiane explained, to celebrate an Austrian victory more than three hundred years ago, driving the invading Turks out of the country. This led to a discussion of the Sachertorte which also had a complicated political and legal history dating back to the time of the Congress of Vienna and to Prince Metternich who, legend had it, wanted a chocolate cake not so rich and gooey, but rather one that would appeal more to a man's taste, something drier. The "original" recipe wound up at Demel's and the other "original" recipe remained at the Sacher Cafe, and for decades the battle raged through the courts, and the entire city of Vienna took sides.

Marge was laughing outright by the time Christiane finished her little history lesson.

"Vienna is a European crossroads," Christiane explained, "and therefore much of our history right down to our pastries, is woven into and out of the culture of other countries."

"I've heard that it is still a hub of European espionage. Is that true?"

"It is. Or, so I have heard. We have always been a city of intrigue, you see, though it is perhaps more sophisticated today than it was in earlier years, now that we have the electronic capacities." She laughed and looked around. "This place, here at the Sacher Cafe, was famous in the years after the war for being the place for buying and selling information. Everyone knew that if you either had or wanted information, you sat at one of these tables," she indicated the two rows of tables that faced each other along the walls and pointed up the aisle between them, "and you ordered coffee. And then, as the waiter left you and walked away, you called after him so as to be heard by others in the café, *'Aber mit Schlag!' Schlagobers* is the whipped cream that may accompany a Viennese coffee but it is optional and must be requested. And this was the universally recognized signal. But you can learn more about these things from the Internet," Christiane said. "I don't wish to bore you."

"You are not boring me."

"Good. And now you must tell me, what have you been doing? What are your plans for the remainder of your visit?"

"I've been just walking around. Reading in the park. I took a ride on the big Ferris wheel, and I went into that old church down by the canal. And saw a couple there, sitting on a bench outside, in the longest kiss I've ever seen. I almost envied them, to be so young. And so oblivious."

"But you are not so old. Surely not old enough to be mourning your lost youth."

"No, of course not. I know. But there are days—" Marge stopped herself. What could be more boring than getting into a big confessional session with a woman she hardly knew? "I've just been working very hard and I guess I'm emotionally a bit vulnerable."

"Ah. Then you must rest. Take a vacation."

"That's just what I'm doing."

"And that is why you are in Vienna?"

"Yes. I spent a couple of weeks in London. I'm not sure if I'm ready to go home, or will spend another couple of weeks resting."

"I will not pry. But I suspect there is a man involved."

Marge laughed. "Worse than that. Two men."

And Christiane laughed, too. "And you must choose?"

"I suppose. It's all happened rather suddenly."

"A whirlwind attraction? A 'shipboard' romance?"

"Hardly that. But now it is my turn to say, 'I will not bore you.'"

"And it is not my business. We will not speak of it further. Instead, if I may, I will make a suggestion or two about your remaining days here in Vienna."

"That's very kind of you. I will not be here long enough to do more than see just a few things. And I am supposed to be resting, so I mustn't have too strenuous a schedule."

"Perhaps you will see the Lipizzaner horses. That's easy. You can go into the Reitschule any morning and watch their practice sessions. At the Hofburg palace—it is just steps away from here." Her gesture indicated the street outside the café. "In the old days, one didn't need even to buy a ticket—one just walked in off the street, any morning, and one could sit upstairs in the gallery and watch them being trained. It was a lovely place to pass a half hour or so, perhaps to meet with a friend while those beautiful horses were put through their paces. Such an elegant and unusual setting.

"And then there is Carnuntum—the Roman encampment being excavated up the road, only a little way toward Budapest, and the two amphitheaters a bit further on down the road from there. And I think the most extraordinary thing about those amphitheaters is that they are just there. Right out in the field. Just as the Roman soldiers left them two thousand years ago, and you can freely walk around in them. When I was a child, we sometimes had our history lessons there, along with a picnic lunch, on the very banks of the Danube. And the teacher would point across the river and tell us about the scary German tribes 'just over there,' she would say, the enemy forces massed against the Roman soldiers who were stationed there to protect this outpost of their empire. It was very exciting. And the boys would play gladiator, exploring in the tunnels and play-fighting out in the arena." Christiane's eyes were alight at the memory. "Ah, but that was so long ago. Vienna is different now. This old city is catching up with the rest of the world."

"It is just right for me now. I need less hectic surroundings. At least for a little while longer."

"And then you must get back to your modern, American—dare I say it?—to your rat race?"

"Oh, my work is no rat race. I love my work. That is, perhaps, the problem. I forget how hard I work, how busy I am, and then I wear myself out."

"And you are traveling about Europe, in a leisurely fashion, to take a rest for a few weeks?"

"That's it."

"And when you return, will these men in your life, will they still be a problem or do you think you will have solved them by then?"

Marge laughed. "I'd better have solved them. I'm supposed to be an excellent problem solver. I won't be able to hold my head up if I haven't."

"My dear, you haven't asked for my advice. But I will tell you anyway. I think you must forget them both, forget all your worries, for the time you are here in Vienna. Tomorrow night, let's the two of us go to Grinzing. You must be my guest and I will introduce you to a proper Viennese Heuriger."

"And that is—?"

"The Heurigen are taverns where the new wines, the 'heurige' wines, are sold. In November, the wines from the vineyards outside the city are ready, and the wineries hang a spruce branch over the front door as a sign that they are ready for the Viennese to come to the Heurigen to taste the new wines and celebrate. There will be singing and drinking and it will be fun. Tell me where you are staying, and my driver will pick you up tomorrow evening at eight." And with a big smile, she added, "You may wear jeans. The Heurigen are very informal. And we can drink till dawn, if we like, and watch the sun rise over the hills of Kahlenberg." Her smile was mischievous, but then she said, more soberly, "Though I think that it is not wise for you to drink till dawn. It may be too strenuous for you, if you are regaining your strength."

"It sounds like fun," Marge said. "Maybe not till dawn, but midnight, anyway." They both laughed, and Marge took a pen and a page of paper from her notebook, wrote down her address and phone number and handed it to Christiane. "Tomorrow at eight. I'm looking forward to it."

They chatted some more, and then Christiane looked at her watch, made her excuses, and said she needed to leave.

"Goodbye, my dear," she said. "We will see each other tomorrow evening."

* * * *

At her villa on the Speisingerstrasse in Mauer, Christiane took off her gloves, removed her jacket and settled comfortably onto the sofa in her living room. She took her cell phone from her bag, and texted a message.

Sam, dear. I have met again with your friend. She is lovely and I enjoyed her company. We will go to

*a Heuriger tomorrow evening and I will put in a
good word for you. Good luck.*

> *Thank you, Christiane. If she should mention
> her next port of call, perhaps you'll be willing to
> share that information with me?*

Christiane smiled. This was fun. Partnering with her old friend and "coconspirator." Like the old days. And now, a little matchmaking on his behalf. A happy task, for a change. She scrolled back up through her messages to the one she'd received from Sam only a few days ago.

> *Christiane. A favor, please? A friend will be
> in Vienna, arriving Monday morning. Marge
> Webster—yes, that Marge Webster. Lady Fair
> magazine.*

> *She is taking a medical leave, so is incognito and
> must not be recognized. And she must not know
> that I am interested. But she is traveling alone
> and I worry that she be safe.*

> *I care for this woman, Christiane. So, behind her
> back—please let it remain there—I'm asking that
> you make contact and be there if needed. Yes?*

> *I've suggested Demel's for her first breakfast.
> Have a coffee on me...*

To which Christiane had replied:

> *You sly dog. Turning me into a an old Cupid. But
> of course. I am happy to help, And I don't need to
> ask. I know you and I know your intentions are
> honorable.*

Chapter Twenty-one

Marge followed Christiane's suggestion and took the bus to Carnuntum. The day was perfect for a ride to the countryside, with the air crisp, the sky blue, and the colors of the foliage along the way changing dramatically. At Carnuntum, she decided to give the ruins and the digs and the museum a pass and just take a walk up the road to see the amphitheaters. Christiane was right; there they were, just there. Right out in farmland that stretched as far as she could see, one amphitheater on the right and a little farther on, another on the left, right up on the banks of the Danube. She had picked up a sandwich and a bottle of Orangina before she'd left, and now she unpacked them and sat down on the grassy edge of the more distant amphitheater, looking down into the floor of the arena. There were extensive remnants of stone bleachers, and stone work at the entrance of a tunnel that burrowed into the hill. It really was remarkable that there was no one in sight; she was totally alone, in a great empty place that had been built thousands of years ago and had been simply left, unattended, just there, like a footprint from an ancient time.

She ate her sandwich. She drank the Orangina. The breeze blew gently about her, and there was a scent of the new-cut hay from the field behind her where, off in the distance, a huge stone arch built by those Romans stood alone, like an alien presence from another time, now in the midst of some farmer's acreage. And she thought about the passage of all those centuries, and the warring tribes and the soldiers, deployed here so long ago to protect the borders of their empire. It seemed that all the years wafted over her.

And then, a strange thing happened. As though it were a kind of hallucination—not quite that, but something like—she imagined so vividly a scene down there on the floor of the arena, a scene so real, she gasped. There were two men, stripped bare except for their pants. Suit pants, of course. And no shoes. She recognized the two men, both tall and quite good-looking, and of course she knew instantly that her imagination had conjured up Jerry and Sam, battling each other fiercely, not with swords, but with their fists. And as long as she watched, they fought and they fought, bloodying each other's noses and raising shiners on each other's eyes and beating against each other's torsos, but neither one seemed to be making any headway against the other. Evenly matched? She wasn't totally losing her mind, and she knew they were only fantasies, but she also knew the significance of what she was imagining—that they each had an equal but different claim on her affections.

Damn! She tried to banish them from her imagination, but there they were. Two strong men. Two very attractive men. Two smart and interesting men. And each with a place in her heart.

Damn, she thought again. Look how cute they are. Both of them in great shape. Though she had to admit, Sam was the sexier of the two. But Jerry had a kind of lasting steadiness. So yes, they were evenly matched and in their battle, nothing that either one of them tried to do could wear the other one down.

This is ridiculous, she said to herself. She closed her eyes, and willed them away, out of her sight. Out of her imagination. She opened her eyes and they were gone.

Wow. That was weird.

She didn't need to wonder what it meant. It was clear enough. She was on the horns of a dilemma and Christiane was right. She should just not think about them. Just. Not. Think. About. Them. Marge was a smart woman, and not given to foolishness. She made them disappear. For the time being. She returned down the road to the bus stop and took the next bus back to Vienna. And congratulated herself on escaping that little time warp.

The bus left her off in front of the Hilton and on her way back to the *Pension Kreindl*, she stopped at a *gasthaus* just off the Singerstrasse and had the best—and the largest—wienerschnitzel she'd ever eaten, large enough to cover the entire plate, with slices of lemon on the edge and a side order of delicious buttery boiled and parsleyed potatoes. Then she went up to her room at the *pension*, turned on the TV and for a while tried to make out what she was hearing, but she had no German and finally gave up. She read for a while. She thought about the coming day and decided to again follow Christiane's suggestion and go to the Reitschule and watch the white Lipizzaner horses. Then she turned out the light and slept. And again, dreamt of the two men, in battle against each other. Still evenly matched. But now, in her dream, there was also a beautiful white stallion, a powerful war horse, trained for combat, tethered at the edges of the arena, impatiently stamping his hooves into the soft earth, waiting to see which man would get to be his rider, which man would scoop her up and take her off into the future.

Damn!

Chapter Twenty-two

She awoke to a rainy day, moody and gray, a good day for indoor activities. Her dream had unsettled her, and it stayed with her, as some dreams do, as the hours of the morning passed. She had a light breakfast at the *pension* and then walked to the Hofburg Palace to watch the horses' training session. By a stroke of luck, just as she approached the palace, she had to stop and wait for a few minutes on the street. The horses were being walked, in single file from their stables across to their entrance into the riding school inside the palace. How often could one be so close to these magnificent animals, close enough, almost, to touch? They had the power, the elegance, and the confidence of champions, and it was exciting to stand there on the street, steps away from them as they passed by her. She felt her day brightening; she bought her ticket and climbed the stairs to the gallery where she could watch their regular morning practice from above.

As brilliant as the horses and their riders were, Marge was equally impressed by their training ground. It seemed to Marge both beautiful and yet strange, that the surface of soft brown earth on which these remarkable animals practiced and performed was inside a palatial hall of gold and gleaming white pillars, enormous French doors, and great crystal chandeliers, with two levels above of galleries for the visitors, and at one end of the hall, a towering painting of the Hapsburg Emperor, Carl VI, whose portrait was ritually saluted by the riders as they entered, each one raising his bicorne hat high as he rode past. Marge felt it was as though ten horses had come into the living room at home to perform among the chairs and the sofa and the coffee table. Yet they were so precisely trained, she knew that not a single bit of damage would—or could—be done by these perfect animals and their perfect riders.

Nor would Marge have been Marge if she hadn't also been exquisitely aware of the details of the riders' uniforms, in each detail a perfection of Empire style, from the double breasted, stiff-collared brown cutaway tail coats, their fronts cropped waist-high and with a row of six gold buttons on each side down the front, to their Napoleon-style bicorne hats with gold braid over a pleated black cockade. Black boots rising at the front above the knee over skin-tight creamy white buckskin breeches. Simple, swan neck spurs, and white deerskin gloves.

She tucked away a mental note to assign someone to do a piece in *Lady Fair* about the style of these riders. They were deliciously beautiful.

She watched riders and horses for about an hour, and was then ready to leave. She came out onto the Josephplatz. The rain had eased up into a misty curtain over the city and she found a coffee house where she could take advantage of the Viennese custom and sit undisturbed for hours to read her book. She ordered a knockwurst sandwich, which turned out to be baloney on a small, crusty, delicious semmel roll served with a small dish of mustard, and a large coffee with milk. No one interrupted her for hours and by four o'clock, she had finished her book. She knew there would be food later that evening at the heurige so she ordered only a second coffee and a small omelet which should be enough until Christiane picked her up at eight.

She came out into a bright, lively early evening scene. People were hurrying home from work, hurrying home for dinner, hurrying out to meet friends. The mist had cleared and the streets, still just a bit damp, reflected lights from the street lamps as well as from the moon which was just coming up over the Stephansdom. She walked back to the *pension* where, because the evening's entertainment promised to go late, she decided to take a little nap. By the time Christiane's driver had the concierge ring up to say they were ready for her, she'd slept a bit, wakened and washed up, dressed in a soft, cotton skirt she'd picked up at a stall in the Naschmarkt a couple of days earlier, a white peasant blouse and her denim jacket, and she was ready for an evening at a heurige.

She and Christiane must have progressed to the next level of friendship because, as she got into the back seat of the car, Christiane greeted her with the traditional air kiss, right cheeks touching first, then left. Christiane's perfume was a blend Marge could not recognize, and she realized it was probably custom made. She sat back into the deep leather seat and prepared to enjoy the evening.

"I've decided," Christine said, "we will not go to Grinzing. The world has discovered Grinzing and you would see only a tricked-out performance for tourists of what a heuriger evening used to be. Instead, I've told Otto," she indicated the driver, "to take us back to Mauer. That is my neighborhood, and we will go to a genuine winery where I know the owner and you will have a more authentic and a more enjoyable heuriger experience. If nothing else, a heuriger evening should be fun. Not a forced imitation of what a tourist imagines it to be."

It was a drive of about twenty minutes, and on the way Christiane gave her a bit of background about the winery's owner, Martin Edlbau, who, she said, had been to school with her son and had inherited the winery when his father died. This was the first Marge had heard a word about Christiane's personal life and soon they were sharing family stories. By the time they arrived at the Edlbau Weingut, a short distance up the hill from the Mauerhauptplatz, Marge and Christiane were on their way to becoming confidantes.

That would come, in fact, after a couple of hours in a traditionally *gemütlich* and rustic heurige setting, with wine groves rising in the hills around them and the *lokal* set at their base. The evening was too cool to stay outdoors where foliage formed a canopy over tables and chairs, unoccupied now. Inside, where the merriment was in progress, the long wood tables were rough-hewn, strangers sat and drank and sang together to lively fiddle and soulful zither music, with everyone joining in. There was also much eating of goulash and potatoes, and drinking of the new wine, which was excellent, and by eleven o'clock, when some folks started to leave and the place became a little quieter, Marge was just a bit buzzed. Not drunk, of course. Marge never got drunk. Christiane had assured her Otto would get her home safely, and she was happy, relaxed, and a little sentimental.

"I'll be sorry to leave Vienna," she said. "You've made this city such a pleasure and these have been good days. When I travel, it's always for work and I never have time to look around and see more than the busy rush around me."

Christiane looked at her thoughtfully for a moment. Then she said, "Marge, I have a confession to make. When I first met you, I said you looked familiar. I have said nothing since then, but now I must tell you, I have in fact realized who you are. Please forgive me that I said nothing, because I realized you didn't want to be recognized." She held up a hand because she saw the shadow that passed over Marge's face. "Do not be disturbed. Even here in Vienna, we do see the international papers and magazines, and though you are usually in a more formal or public setting, your face is very familiar to any woman who pays attention to her appearance. No, no, do not be angry. I have so much enjoyed meeting you, and I would not want to make you uncomfortable."

"I'm not angry," Marge said. "How could I be angry? You've been such a treat. I was just startled. I thought I was doing a pretty good job of hiding." She laughed lightly. "As long as you don't blow my cover. I trust you to keep my secret."

"Of course. You have your reasons and it is none of my business."

"Well, it's really just that I've been working too hard and my doctor insisted on my taking a leave—just disappear and rest and recuperate. But if it's reported in the media that Marge Webster hasn't been feeling well, the stock market reacts. And we can't have that, can we?"

"What a burden to carry on such young shoulders."

"Oh, I'm used to it. I don't mind. But I have to think of shareholders and the magazine's staff, and et cetera. And you know, it really has been fun, in a way, this cloak and dagger stuff. I've been feeling sort of invisible, like a fly on the wall, just observing. Except there's been one problem. Well, I don't know if I should call it a problem. Exactly."

"Yes?"

"Well," she drank some more of the wine in her glass, "the thing is, I've been found out by someone else—"

"Someone besides me?"

"He knew me already. But he found out where I was and he spent some time with me, and—" She sighed. A big, satisfied sigh that spoke a great deal. "And actually, it was very nice. Really very nice. But I made him go away, because there is this other person—"

"Oh, my dear. Men do make such a mess of our lives, don't they?"

"Yes, a mess. But also, they are so necessary. And sometimes, so nice." She drank the rest of the wine in her glass and filled it again from the bottle on the table. And drank a bit more. "So I told him to go away, and we agreed that if I want him to come again, I would write to him and tell him."

"And you want to write to him?"

"I want to write to both of them. I miss them both."

"Oh, that is a problem."

"Yes, it is. They're both such good guys. But different. Very different." She sipped a bit more of her wine. "I've been thinking of going to Paris. Do you think Paris would be a good place to make a decision? I have a friend who has a nice little pied à terre near the *Rue Cler*. She's always said I can use it if ever I want to. Paris is such a beautiful city, and I've always wanted so much to just wander around and be lazy and sit at a sidewalk cafe and watch people go by and just walk and walk and walk and see it as ordinary folks do. But I spend so much time there, my face is known to many people. What do you think? I could wear a disguise. I could grow a mustache."

Christiane laughed.

"No, really," Marge said. "I could do something to hide my face. Or wear a wig. Cut my hair into bangs. Something."

"My dear," Christiane said, "Paris is a lovely, romantic place for managing affairs of the heart. But you are a little tipsy and the wine is guiding you. That's not wise. But if I may, I will offer you one tiny bit of advice."

Marge took a big, deep breath, willing herself to be *not* tipsy and to focus her attention. "I'm listening," she said. "Seriously, Christiane. I am listening."

Christiane laid a hand over Marge's. "My dear, go to Paris if you like and enjoy your stay there, but when you make your choice, you must choose the man who makes you happy. It is that simple."

Marge looked deep into Christiane's bright gray eyes. Then she lifted her glass. "I will definitely drink to that." She had a couple more sips, put down the glass, and said, "Now all I need to do is figure out which of the two makes me happier."

Christiane laughed. "Oh, my dear. You are afflicted with a surfeit of good choices. So difficult." She took a bit of bread, broke off a piece, buttered it, ate it, and said, "And if you do decide to go to Paris, please let me know where you'll be. I would like so much to stay in touch."

"Of course."

"And now, because it is almost midnight, and I must get my beauty rest, I will have Otto drive me home first—it is a short way from here—and then he will take you back to Vienna."

She settled up the bill, Marge thanked her for a wonderful evening and for excellent advice, Christiane texted Otto to tell him to bring the car around, and soon they were pulling up to the tall iron gate at Christiane's villa. Otto waited until she'd gotten herself inside and locked the gate behind her, and then he took Marge back into town.

* * * *

And while Otto was driving Marge back into town, Christiane took a moment to text to Sam:

*She is going to Paris. Some little place near the
Rue Cler. Will let you know when and exactly
where.*

I think your chances are good.

She likes you.

> *Bless you, Christiane. She's wonderful, isn't she?*

Yes, dear. I like her very much.

Chapter Twenty-three

She woke up laughing. Every now and then, her dreams told her a joke, and this one was a doozy. There was this enormous open field. Very green and very bright and summery, with mountains in the distance and fluffy white clouds up above in a blue, blue sky. A very happy scene. And the white horses were there, a whole herd of gorgeous Lipizzaners, and they were running every which way, tails flying, manes tossing. And, believe it or not, they were laughing. Big, whinnying horse-laughs. And the reason they were laughing was that Jerry and Sam were also there in the dream, both of them, and they were running after the horses, trying to catch them, but the horses were much too clever and much too fast to be caught. They twisted this way and that, pretending to be almost caught and then with a quick side-step and a leap, they'd be off again, still elusive. And the funniest thing about it was that both men were in very proper business suits—white dress shirts, ties, Jerry in his best blue pinstripe and Sam in charcoal grey—both of them running wildly and both of them very red in the face.

"It must have been the wine," she said to the mirror as she brushed her teeth. "I put away almost half a bottle all by myself."

But she didn't feel at all fuzzy. Not at all. She felt perfectly clear and in a very good mood. A quick shower, and two minutes to get into a tee shirt, jeans, Top-Siders, and her denim jacket. She pulled her hair up into a pony tail, twisted it around, and secured it into a scraggly knot with a tortoise shell hair stick. A dash of lipstick, and she was ready to go. And all the while, thinking about last night. About Christiane's advice.

"Can it really be that simple? Is it just a matter of who makes me happy?"

She went down to the dining room, a small room just off the lobby, where breakfast was still being served. She ordered a soft boiled egg which was served in an egg cup. The egg was wearing an embroidered little cap to keep it warm and that little cap added to Marge's happy mood. It was such a pretty little thing, with peasant figures dancing around it. She made a mental note to find out where she could buy some. There were also butter curls on her bread plate along with a couple of *kipferl*. The coffee was in a silver pot and a small pitcher of boiled milk came with it. She felt well-cared-for.

And it was in that mood that she finished her breakfast and left the dining room, eager for the day. She stopped at the concierge's desk to ask about the egg cup cozies.

The concierge took a tourist map from a drawer and with a pen, marked a place on the map. "We buy ours from a commercial hotel supply firm, but you should be able to find some very nice ones here," as she pointed with her pen. "Here, near Am Hof, where the Tuchlauben and the Bognergasse meet. There's a linen shop on the corner. I'm sure you can find something lovely there."

But she decided to put off shopping at the linen shop till later in the day. Egg cozies could wait. The day was too pretty to be anywhere but in the open air. The Stadtpark was only a short walk from the *pension*, and when she got there, she went looking for a good place to sit and think. Think about what she would be doing next. Think about what Christiane had said to her. She stopped wandering around the park when she found an inviting bench facing a playground. She took a notebook and pen out of her bag, opened it up, turned to the next blank page, and drew a line down the center. At the top of the column on the left, she wrote, in big black letters:

JERRY

And of course, in the right-hand column, she wrote:

SAM

Then she divided each column into subcolumns, "pro" and "con."
And at the bottom of each, she wrote, "Makes me happy?"
And then she stared at the page for a long time without writing anything. She was distracted by the children.

By the sound of their playing, their laughter and shrieks and calls to each other. By the mothers and nannies and, presumably, grandmas, telling them to be careful, to watch out, "Don't climb so high," "Play nicely," "Come here, you need to blow your nose," "Stop fighting." At least, that's what she guessed they were saying. Even in German, she was sure they must be saying, "Yes, I was watching, I saw what you did." And the universal "Good job!"

The children held her attention. She was charmed by their liveliness, by their innocence, by their nimbleness. They were incredibly darling, in their little jeans and tiny tee shirts and Nike sneakers. And she had to laugh at herself, because she found it remarkable that they could chatter in fluent, melodious, bird-like German—*so young and they already know German*—as though it was a marvel that they spoke a foreign language. Which was silly, of course, and she knew it was silly, but that's what passed through her head.

For a long time, she watched them, pretended she could figure out everything about them, the personalities of each, how each would grow up, just from the way they played. One little girl in a sandbox was working hard to help a younger child fill up a pail. Another was slapping the hand of a little boy, preventing him from taking her toy from her. One fearless little girl was hanging upside down from a large, complicated, jungle gym sort of structure. Two boys were tussling and a third, an older one, made them break it up, made them shake hands and get back to their game.

Funny, how little boys learn early to shake and get over it. Girls hold grudges to the death. A girl will say, "I hate her guts and I'll never talk to her again."

It reminded her of what she'd said to Bridey—was it only a few weeks back? How long ago that seemed, back in September and an ocean and a continent away.

Whatever it is the boys are experiencing here in the playground, they always want to come back to it. And the girls, not so much.

She wondered why that was so.

Well, she thought, *I can't figure out that one, but about Jerry and Sam, I do have to come to a conclusion.* She forced her attention back to her notebook.

It really didn't take that long. After a half hour, here's what she had:

JERRY
pro: con:

good guy; goes on and on when he explains things
works hard okay in bed—(but magic?)
successful; impossible at fixing things, can't screw in a lightbulb
nice looking
doesn't snore
loves me a lot
remembers my birthday
would never cheat (I think)
would marry me in a minute

At the bottom, where she'd put the question to herself: "Makes me happy?" she wrote:

"Well, he's never made me unhappy."

And that was the left-hand side of the page.
On the right side, this is what she had after a half hour:

SAM

pro: con:
good guy—I think
works hard—I think
successful—apparently
nice looking
knew me way back when
persistent!!!

Nothing at all on the "con" side.
Instead, she wrote right across his column:

"Insufficient information!
I hardly know anything about Sam now. He was a good guy back in high
school, but that was long ago.
Does he snore?
Would he bore me to tears explaining some minor point of the law?
Handy with a screwdriver? I suspect yes, but I don't know.
What was that about "military intelligence" and the buddy who finagled
something to help him find me? Good thing? Bad thing?
And in bed—"

She paused there, because she felt a little tingle right in the corner of her mouth—

and then wrote:

—I'd bet anything sex with Sam would be great!

She stared for a long time at what she'd written. Then, with a huge sigh, she looked up from her notebook. And watched the children some more.

And then looked back at her list and was shocked to realize she'd written nothing about either man as a father. For years she'd felt there wasn't much room in her life for children and just put it off as something to think about in the future. But now, with this list in front of her, and the little ones running and laughing only steps away from her, it hit her like a smack in the face: this really was something she had to think about.

Would she ever have her own little ones running about in a playground somewhere? Would she ever be the one sitting on a park bench, calling, "Good job" every time they took a step? Would she ever have the fun of choosing a car seat, or sheets for a baby's bed, or dressing them in precious little outfits, those tiny shoes and little bitty socks, or "kissing it better" when they hurt a finger, or struggling to get them into good schools, or driving herself crazy trying to be a perfect parent? Was she in danger of delaying so long, being so preoccupied with her work that the possibilities would just slip by until it was too late? These next few years would be the crucial ones.

Jerry never talked to her about having kids. But she was sure he'd be a good father. Steady and serious and thoughtful. And committed. Probably.

And Sam? She remembered the way he was back in school. He was the one who broke up all the fights. He was the one who knew how to be serious, but with a light touch. Adolescents were so volatile and Sam always knew how to steer everyone through their disputes to a good solution. Was that a sign about parenting?

She thought of him at the Peter Pan statue. Keeping his youth alive.

She wished there was a way to test men to predict their fathering skills. And how many men test really well—and then fail tragically when it comes to the real thing?

Jerry would go out and play catch in the back yard with his sons, and probably his daughters, too—because that's what good fathers do.

Sam would play catch because playing catch was fun.

She was pretty sure of that.

But did "playing catch" matter?

She watched the children for a long, long time. She imagined being responsible for a child's future. She'd felt the hunger for a baby before this day, but always set it aside, putting it off to "another time; not now." Why was now, this day, different? Was it because she was sitting here, watching these real-life kids? Were they ramping up her maternal juices? Was it the little toddler who'd come over to her, curious, with his plump round cheeks and his searching blue eyes, looking deeply and innocently into her eyes—*my God, how open and innocent and precious each baby is*—or was it his awkward "bye bye" gesture as he looked back at her, curling his little fingers in an effort to do it right as his mommy drew him away with a murmur of apology? Was this what made her heart twist in longing? Or was it because she was facing a very grown-up choice between two men? Thinking about opening up her life and future to one of them?

There she was, on a bench in a park in a foreign country, watching some children who had no connection at all to her, listening to their chatter that was incomprehensible to her. And now, now at this moment and for the very first time, she really longed to be a mommy.

Chapter Twenty-four

She was crying when she left the park. What had happened to this day that had started out so well? She went back to the *pension*, washed her face and then sat at the little vanity table for a while, looking into the mirror, and she had a little talk with herself.

"Marge, this is more serious than you realized. Whatever you decide about these two men, there's going to be a big change in your life. It's time to face up to it. And you can't decide at a distance. You're going to have to confront each of them. But it can't be done now. Not yet. You need to get yourself settled down first. Go out. Have lunch. Do a little shopping. That always helps."

She made a face at herself in the mirror, reassured herself that the world was not coming to an end, and went out to find some lunch.

There was a cute little *Beisl* just around the corner on the Wollzeile that she'd been meaning to try, so this seemed to be a good time. Lunch would help her postpone any decisions. After a bowl of soup—a rich chicken soup with hunks of chicken and short skinny noodles and an egg threaded through it, like a Chinese egg drop soup—and dark bread cut thick on which she slathered the great butter that seemed to be everywhere, followed by apricot *Palatschinken*—which turned out to be crepes layered with jam—and some more great coffee—she was ready to go out and face the world. At least, face the little corner of it where she was.

She had just paid the bill and had walked out into the sunshine, when her phone signaled a message.

It had been silent all these weeks. An emergency?

It was Jerry. No, no emergency. Not really.

*Hi Marge. I know you're hiding somewhere. But I
wanted to tell you, the case is done. My guy came
out OK, but the others are facing heavy fines.
Your friend Sam is tough. Can you come home
soon? I miss you. You OK?*

She stared at her phone for a long time.
So the case is finished. They're free now to get back to—whatever.

She imagined the two men in the same room together all those weeks,
facing each other every day, with Sam knowing where she was, knowing
that he'd been with her in London. And the whole time, every day, Jerry
in the dark. It was so unfair. And so unkind to Jerry, who always played
by the rules.

What to do?

She sighed. She'd decide later. She put her phone into the pocket of her
jacket—and found there the little slip of paper with the name of the linen
shop on the Tuchlauben. She'd go there. Buy egg cozies. A souvenir of
her time here in Vienna. She consulted her map. Only a few streets away.
She'd be there in maybe ten minutes.

What she found at the Tuchlauben surprised her. Centuries-old buildings
updated to accommodate high end flagship stores. As though her home
turf had followed her, here were Jimmy Choo and Chanel, Prada and
Louis Vuitton and Alexander McQueen. And more. And looking snazzy
and totally *au courant* right in the heart of Vienna's old inner city, a place
that had been already ancient two thousand years ago when the Romans
arrived and created Vindobona on top of a primitive Celtic settlement.

Tucked away on an unobtrusive corner, she found the shop she was
looking for, a small gift shop specializing in fine needlepoint, and she
spent a happy half hour there, examining linens and embroidery work,
fine batiste nightgowns and handkerchiefs—and the cozies she'd come
to buy, they looked like tiny ski caps, thick and padded and embroidered
with hearts and flowers and peasant girls dressed in dirndls. She chose a
dozen of varying designs and was about to pay for them, taking the bills
out of her wallet, when the sales clerk said, "It's been a pleasure to serve
you, Ms. Webster. And an honor to have you in our little shop. I had no
idea you were in Vienna. I hope you are enjoying your stay here."

Marge stared at her.

Oh my God, I've been recognized!

Of course. She had stumbled into the very part of town where it was most likely that her face would be familiar, even if her "disguise" was a raggedly pinned pony tail and jeans and a tee shirt.

She stammered something awkward and got out of there as fast as she could.

She longed for a paper bag to put over her head, and hoped, as she walked past Louis Vuitton and Chanel and the others, that she could get back to the *Pension Kreindl*—and then get out of Vienna as fast as she could, like a thief in the night. Well, not quite in the night. She'd call Bridey right away to be sure it was okay to stay in her place in Paris, and then leave first thing in the morning. But word would be out in the high fashion part of town that Marge Webster, supposedly "on vacation," was right here in Vienna and dressed like an unrecognizable American tourist, and reporters from *W* and the *International Times* and God knows who else would be chasing her for a story.

By eight o'clock in the morning, she'd check out and be on the early train heading west. No Orient Express on this trip, no exposure to luxury class. She'd book a single compartment, and just hide out all the way through Switzerland and France. And she'd have to be more careful in Paris. At least she knew Paris well enough to know where *not* to go.

* * * *

Back in her room at the *pension*, she locked the door, as though hordes of pursuers might be trying to break in. She checked her watch. Six hours' time difference; not too early to call Bridey.

"I'm fine. I'm fine," she said. "Oh, but Bridey, I have so much to tell you. You'll die. It's been fascinating. But not now. Not till I get back. Now, Bridey, you have to promise—absolutely *promise*—not a word to anyone. Not even to Mack. Not even to the children. Not even to those precious cats of yours. You understand? You promise?"

"Of course."

"You have to say it. You have to say you promise."

"Oh, Marge, you sound like a twelve-year-old. Of course I promise. What is it?"

"I want to go to Paris. And absolutely no one—I mean *no one*—can know I'm there. And I'm calling to ask if I can use your place."

"Of course you can. How long? When will you be getting there?"

"Tomorrow afternoon."

"No problem. Do you remember Mme. Michou? The old concierge? She's retired now. I'll call the new concierge, Mme. Pilard, and tell her to give you the key. It'll be fine. She won't recognize you at all. You remember the address?"

"Yes, I have it. On the corner, at the *Square Robiac.*"

"That's it. And what name should I tell her?"

"Oh, I hadn't thought of that. I'm not really good at this cloak and dagger stuff." She thought a moment. Then said, "Just tell her I'm Ms. Adams. That's simple enough."

"Marge, are you okay? You sound—sort of—weird."

"I'm okay. I really am. And we'll have plenty to talk about when I see you."

"When are you coming home?"

"Probably in a couple of weeks."

"Are you feeling better? Getting enough rest? Eating right?"

"Actually, I am feeling better. In fact, I'm feeling *much* better. And I'm feeling good about getting back to work. Dr. Diaz will be pleased. I'm eating like a horse. You don't need to worry. I'm fine. But it's all been a little more interesting than I'd anticipated. Maybe a lot more interesting."

"Can't wait to hear it all. You take care, Marge, you hear? Gotta go now. Kids yelling. How do they know the minute I'm on the phone?"

"Kids have magic powers." *Boy, do they ever!* "Bye, sweetie. Kisses to them both. And hi to Mack. Love ya. And thanks for your pad in Paris. I'll take good care of it."

* * * *

She was too preoccupied with her own hurried change of schedule, and didn't remember, till she was on the train to Paris, that she'd told Christiane Riemer she'd let her know where she'd be staying. She took out her phone and texted her Paris contact information to her, with a nice little message to thank her for making her time in Vienna so pleasant.

Chapter Twenty-five

Mme. Pilard took the key off a hook on the wall and handed it over to Marge. She spoke no English, and Marge's French was rudimentary, but with signs and smiles and good will, they managed to communicate. Marge said, "*Merci bien*," left Mme. Pilard in her apartment, and climbed the cool marble steps. Bridey's Paris pied à terre was up a couple of flights and Marge was eager to get the door closed behind her. It had been a thirteen-hour trip from Vienna, and she just wanted to drop her carry-on, wash up and then go out, find a bistro nearby, and have some dinner.

She'd been there before, a couple of years earlier, when Bridey and Mack had taken a little vacation in Paris at the same time that she'd been there for Fashion Week. They'd had only a couple of hours together, but she remembered a beautiful little hideaway, tiny but comfortable and exquisitely redone to modernize the kitchen, which was really just a counter along one wall, with built-in sink, fridge, and stove, with cabinets above and below, where Bridey, being the super chef that she was, could put together a gourmet meal with all the trimmings on just those rudimentary appliances. The bath was tucked away in a separate room with a huge and very modern shower and tub. Marge promised herself a good soak later on.

In moments, she was out on the street, and walked over to the *Rue Cler*. It was a street rich in cafés and bistros, but she was so hungry, she went into the very first bistro she passed, where she had an excellent dinner of roast chicken and potatoes with a glass of wine and ice cream for dessert. And she was back in the apartment by ten, had a long soak in the tub. And went to bed and slept long and well.

* * * *

If she dreamt any dreams that night, she didn't remember them in the morning when she woke up just after eight o'clock. But before she'd even brushed her teeth, she saw that she had a message. And this one was from Jerry.

Another one from Jerry. Second message in just a couple of days. He knows I'd asked the whole world to leave me alone till I got back. What is this?

> *I had a call from Sam Packard.*

> *He wanted to meet with me. I had an awful hour with him.*

> *You and I have to talk. Call me.*

Oh, God!

She checked; the message had arrived at 4:53 a.m., while she was sleeping. Six hours' time difference between Paris and New York. He must have sent his text just before 11:00 p.m. in New York. She checked her watch. It was now 2:00 a.m. in New York. He'd still be sleeping.

Oh, God!

But maybe not. A silent text wouldn't waken him. She texted him.

> *Are you sleeping?*

No answer came back. So yes, he was sleeping. She'd have to wait until the afternoon to call him.

This is awful. What could Sam have said to him?

She brushed her teeth. She brushed her hair. She walked around the tiny apartment, like an animal in a cage. She brushed her hair some more.

The phone rang.

Before she could even say "hello," she heard, "Where are you?"

"Jerry?"

"Yes, it's me. Where are you?"

"Where are *you*?"

"I'm here. I'm sitting in a café on the corner. The damn concierge wouldn't let me in. Said there was no Marge Webster there." He sounded pissed.

She stared at the phone as though it had grown a head. Her mouth was open but no words came out.

"Damn it, Marge. I'm in no mood. I haven't slept, I've been on a plane all night, little kid next to me, cried the whole way. Jesus! And now, I can't find you. Where are you?"

Her voice returned. "I'm here. I'll come down. Which café?"

There was a pause. Then he said, "Café Larroche. On the *Rue Grenelle*."

And he was gone. She stared at the phone some more. Then she washed her face, put on some clothes, and went downstairs.

* * * *

He looked disheveled and also a little gray, like a man who needed a good night's sleep. And he was definitely looking not happy. He stood up as she came in.

"I'm not sure," he said. "Is it okay to kiss you hello?"

"Oh, Jerry. Don't be silly." She put a hand on his arm and held her face up to him.

His kiss was perfunctory. "I wasn't sure."

She sat down.

"You look awful," she said.

"Damn kid never stopped crying all the way over. And then he threw up all over his mother. God, what a mess."

She had to laugh. "I know," she said, apologetically. "It's not funny. I shouldn't laugh."

"Have you had breakfast? Should I order something?"

"I just got up. I wasn't even dressed when you called." She pointed to the coffee in front of him and said, "Just coffee, thanks." Jerry signaled the waiter who came right over with a cup and silver pitcher of coffee on a small tray. He poured it out for her and they were silent until he left.

And continued to be silent for a long time, while Jerry stared at her and she wished she could avoid his eyes. Finally, he spoke.

"You got my message?"

"I did."

Another very long silence.

Then Jerry said, "Leave it to you to give me a rival who's a good guy."

"You're both good guys, Jerry."

He nodded, agreeing. "That makes it harder. If either one of us was a rat, at least we could hope the good guy wins."

"I didn't mean for this to happen."

"I know. At least, that's what Sam tells me."

"Just what did he tell you?"

"He told me how it was between you two, long ago. That you broke up in some stupid adolescent way and that when he ran into you in the courthouse, it broke his heart all over again. And when he saw you and me together in the restaurant, he decided to make his move. And then he chased you down in London."

"That's about the way it was."

"I wish he hadn't done it while we were litigating this thing between us all these weeks. It makes me feel like a fool."

"I'm sorry."

"And he said you sent him away."

"I did."

"But I had the feeling it wasn't all platonic and hands-off between you, there in London."

"What did he tell you?"

"Not much. Just a feeling I had."

She sat quietly, thoughtfully, trying to decide how much to share. Jerry waited while she sorted out her thoughts.

"I didn't sleep with him, Jerry." She'd decided she was willing to say that much.

"I'm not sure it would have made much difference if you had. Something happened between you. I can tell that much." He reached across the table, put his hand over hers. "Marge, we've been together for six years. Almost seven, now."

"I know, Jerry. But we never said we were exclusive, that there couldn't be others."

"There haven't been others for me, Marge. Never. In all these years. And I guess I thought that was true for you, too."

She laughed, briefly. "I've probably been too damn busy. But it's true, there hasn't been anyone else for me either, in all these years."

"So, is this just a fling? Is it going to blow over? Where do I stand?"

"Oh, Jerry. I don't know what it is. I just don't know." She felt so sad for him—as much as for herself. She realized he'd been blindsided, that it was only hours ago that this had all fallen in on him. "You look exhausted. Did you book a room?" She brushed her hand against his hair, straightening it a bit.

"No, I just went right to the airport and took the next flight to Paris. And by the way, how did Sam know where you were? He gave me that address on the Robiac. The one I went to where the concierge wouldn't let me in. She said you weren't there. Never heard of you. And for that matter, how was he able to find you in London? Everyone knew you didn't want people tracking you down, that you needed your rest and isolation. Even I didn't know where you were. When you left, nobody knew where you were going. Not even Bridey knew where you were headed; I asked her and she hadn't a clue."

"I know how he found me in London. He told me. Well, he didn't tell me much, but he said he'd had some intelligence experience in the military, after law school, and I had the impression he has a network of useful friends everywhere. He did some sleuthing, and then an old buddy in London helped him out." She stopped there. Then she said, asking herself the question, "But how did he know where to find me in Paris? I didn't tell anyone—" She stopped herself. "Oh, my God. I did tell someone." She remembered texting her contact information to Christiane Riemer, so glad she'd remembered to do that before she got to Paris, with a nice little thank you note. And with that, she also remembered Christiane at the Sacher Café, talking about post-war intrigue in Vienna and old spy networks and new ones, too. How did Christiane know to be in Demel's her first morning in Vienna? Then she remembered Sam's last words to her as he rode off in that taxi on Bayswater Road: *"Have your first breakfast at Demel's. On the Kohlmarkt."* She didn't know if she should be furious—or charmed. James Bond couldn't have been any smoother. "Maybe Sam Packard really does have 'old buddies' everywhere. And they come in all shapes, sizes—and ages and genders."

"What do you mean?"

"Never mind. I'll save that for another time. It's a good story."

"I suppose I should thank the guy for being honest enough to come to me with the truth. It was the honorable thing for him to do. It couldn't have been easy."

"Yes." She was remembering, from the old days. Sam seemed always to have a code of ethical behavior. Even when he was just a kid.

"So what do we do now?"

"I don't know."

"Look, Marge. I'm not going to sit here and drink coffee all day. I haven't slept. I'm mad. And I want to be alone with you."

Well, fair's fair, she thought.

"Okay, Jerry. You need to get some rest. Come on up to the apartment. You can get some sleep there."

Chapter Twenty-six

Mme. Pilard frowned at Jerry as she saw them go past her apartment and up the stairs, but she said nothing.

"She thinks I'm Miss Adams," Marge whispered to him. "Emphasis on the 'Miss.' If I'd known you were coming, I'd have warned you."

Jerry just shook his head, choosing to ignore Mme. Pilard's disapproval. He looked up the long spiral stairway. "Is it a big climb?" he asked. "I'm beat," he said.

"Two flights."

"Okay. Lead the way."

The bed in the little pied à terre took up most of the available space, and Jerry looked at it fondly. "But first," he said, "I feel filthy. That damn kid on the plane. I stayed out of his way, but still—" He sort of shuddered. "I need a shower."

"In there," Marge said, pointing. "I think there are new toothbrushes in the cabinet over the basin."

He was gone for not more than ten minutes and came out with wet hair slicked back, a bath towel wrapped around his middle, and looking for a place to put his clothes.

She was about to take them from him, "Here, I'll hang them up—" but he dropped them on a chair and put his arms around her.

"Never mind about that," he said. He pulled her close. He smelled of toothpaste and soap. "You're not going to send me away, are you?"

"Oh, Jerry. Of course not. I'm glad you're here." She realized that it was true. She *was* glad. Maybe, with some time alone with Jerry, she'd be able to sort things out.

"Marge, honey." He was so close and he was looking at her so intently, so lovingly, his eyes seeming to be drinking in every feature of her face, as though he were memorizing every bit of it, "This must be confusing for you." With one hand, he caressed her hair, stroking it back from her forehead. "I'm not blaming you. He's an appealing guy. And he's a change. I'm the one you've grown accustomed to. I understand. I can't dazzle you anymore. Maybe I never could. But it never was that way between us. It was just—I don't know—it was just a 'good thing' between us. Steady and regular and comfortable. That can't be a bad thing, can it?"

"Oh, Jerry, of course not. It's not a bad thing at all. It's a good thing."

"You know I love you. You know I'd marry you in a minute if that's what you wanted."

She felt her heart melting. He was so sweet. And so decent.

"Let's not try to decide anything now," she said. "You're exhausted and you need to sleep."

"Not that exhausted," he said. "It's been weeks, and I've missed you so much."

She was completely willing when he kissed her. It was a long kiss and a kiss that became deeper and more passionate as each moment passed. She could feel the pulse of his heart, and she knew her own heart was responding. He reached up under her tee shirt and unhooked her bra and she held herself still closer against him. He pulled her down onto the bed with him. And in a moment the towel was gone and her clothes were on the floor, and for the time being, she was able to forget about Sam.

* * * *

Jerry was sound asleep when she got out of the bed and went into the bathroom. She washed up, and then stared into her own eyes in the mirror.

"Well, Marge," she whispered to herself. "What are you going to do now?"

Chapter Twenty-seven

There were no answers coming back from the mirror and she decided to take a walk and let Jerry sleep. She dressed quietly and tiptoed out. She realized she hadn't eaten all day and it was now after one o'clock. She bought a newspaper and walked to the *Avenue Bosquet* where she found an inviting café. It was too chilly to sit outside, so she found an unobtrusive spot at a table in the corner, ordered a shrimp risotto, and tried to read the paper while she ate. But she kept reading the same paragraph over and over; she was too preoccupied to concentrate on the news.

Was she glad that Jerry was there? Yes? No? She kept going back and forth.

It was only fair, that he get to spend time with her, too. And surely there was a loyalty she owed him—after all these years.

And just because Sam was a real turn-on, an exciting replay from their youth, that didn't exactly make Jerry disposable. Did it?

Did she owe anything to either of them? And what did she owe to herself?

What did she want? She was dismayed to realize she wanted to have Sam sitting there with her so she could discuss her problem with him. And that thought was so bizarre, she was embarrassed even to be thinking it.

She ordered coffee. And that didn't help. She ordered a *tarte tatin*. And then practically cried into it, because she loved a well-prepared *tarte tatin* and this one was excellent, and she was too distracted to enjoy it.

Sam. This is terrible. I really wish you were here.

She had told him, way back in London, that if she wanted him to come to her, she'd let him know.

Remember? That's what you told him.

But that's what she had said when she wanted to keep him away. Now she was thinking that maybe she really didn't want to keep him away. Would he really come if she asked him to? Was it an awful idea to have both men in Paris, with her, at the same time? What was she thinking? She had no idea.

This is idiotic.

> *Sam. I shouldn't do this. Jerry is here. In Paris.*
> *I wish u were here, too. (That's funny—"having*
> *confusing time and wish u were here.")*

> *I'm already regretting writing this –*

There was a pause of a few moments, and Sam's answer came back.

Of course Jerry is in Paris. I figured he would
be.

Never regret, Marge dear.

There was another pause, a little longer, and then a second message from Sam.

Where are u?

> *U shd know. U alwys know where I am*

Not really psychic. ;-)

Tell me.

> *In Paris.*

I know that. Where?

> *Corner Grenelle and Bosquet.*

OK. That's good.

Walk down Grenelle to the Invalides. On the corner, there's a hotel. I'm in the restaurant there.

I'll wait for u.

This was not the first time today she stared at her phone as though it had morphed into a totally new form.
How does he do it?

How do u do it?

I'm magic. Should take u about 10 minutes to get here.

I'll be wearing a red carnation so you'll recognize me.

Oh, I'll know u. Ur the one with the cloak and dagger.

Sorry about that.

I really am sorry.

Don't be mad.

Have you had lunch?

Should I order something?

A glass of wine?

U bet!

She smiled. And started walking.

* * * *

And sure enough, right there on the corner of the *Rue Grenelle*, where it meets the *Place des Invalides*, there was a hotel, and when she went inside to the restaurant, there was Sam, with a wicked smile on his face and a bottle of wine in his hand. He raised it, as though making a toast, and then got up to hold the chair for her.

Silently, he poured out a drink for each of them, and silently they sat for a moment, each examining the other. Then they each began to talk at the same time:

"There's something I have to tell —"

"I know you're wondering—"

And they both laughed. And Sam indicated with a gesture of his hand, "You first."

"Okay," Marge said. "I'm not even sure where to start. First of all, I told you, Jerry is here. In Paris."

"I figured he would be."

"You figured—?"

"He must have told you we'd talked. I'd been feeling like a jerk, all through the trial, knowing I'd been seeing you behind his back, and him not knowing. So when the trial ended, I called him, told him I needed to talk to him, and we met at some little place near his office. And I told him about how I knew you, about us being in high school together, about everything, that we weren't just 'friends.' And that I'd gone to London a couple of times to see you, and that I knew where you were now."

"Yeah," she said. "We'll get to that later. About how you knew where I was. But first tell me, how did you know he'd be here this morning?"

"I saw the look in his eyes. He was plenty mad. And I've watched him work these last few weeks. He's tenacious. I knew he'd be on the next plane."

"And what about you? Why are you here?"

"What I didn't know is if he'd come with guns blazing. If he was in a rage. I don't know the guy that well but I'd seen how determined he could be. I didn't think he'd hurt you, but a man in that situation—" Sam paused. "I just thought it might be a good idea to be nearby." He reached over and put his hand over hers. "Marge, I know I promised not to show up unless you wrote and told me to. But I hoped, with Jerry here, you would *want* me to be here, too. I hoped you would write. And I thought it would be a good idea to be already here just in case you did." His phone was on the table, at one side, and he picked it up so she could see the chain of text messages that they'd exchanged only minutes earlier. "And look," with a big smile, "you did."

"And what would you have done if I hadn't written?"

"I'd have waited a couple of days and if I didn't hear from you, I'd just go on back to New York with my tail between my legs. But I know Jerry's firm has another big case beginning on Monday and he's lead counsel on that one, so he'll have to be back by then." Sam laughed. "You sure are messing us up. How's a man supposed to concentrate on his job when he's chasing you all around the globe?"

"What about you?"

"I've got a break for a few weeks. Not a problem for me."

"Lucky you."

"So where's Jerry now?"

"He's sleeping."

"Sleeping, eh?"

Yes, Sam. Jerry's sleeping. In my bed. And I know what you're thinking.

Yes, of course, she knew what Sam was thinking, what he wanted to know. He was examining her face so closely, he could have been measuring it for a mask—as though maybe he could find the answer in her eyes—but he was a gentleman and he wouldn't ask.

You men! Yes, Sam. We were in bed together. We had sex. He made love to me. And I'm not going to give him a grade.

But she might as well have spoken her thoughts aloud. Because Sam stopped studying her face, and clearly had found his answer. Yes, they did understand each other very easily.

And together, they both said, "So what do we do now?"

And together they laughed.

"We finish our wine," Sam said.

"And you get to tell me how you knew where I am. It was Christiane, wasn't it?"

"Yeah. It was Christiane. How did you guess?"

"It wasn't much of a guess. She's the only one I told where I was going. Is she another one of your 'old buddies'?"

"She's quite a woman, isn't she? She goes back a long way, long before my time. Back to the war years."

"She's very smooth. I was completely taken in."

"Don't be mad at her. I owe a lot to her. I'll tell you someday."

"Okay, Sam. I won't be mad at her. But I am mad at you. I can't believe you've been spying on me."

"Well, not exactly spying."

"What do you mean, 'not exactly?' That's exactly what you've been doing."

"I was just using my resources. It's what I do when I need information. You weren't mad when I found you in London. When I pulled you out of that crowd at Speakers Corner."

He looked so sheepish, her heart went out to him. She couldn't help herself.

"Oh, Sam. What can I say? I should be so angry."

"Will it help if I promise I'll never, *never* do it again?"

She sighed and shrugged her shoulders. Why was it so easy to forgive this man?

"At least," he added, "I promise that *your* secrets will always be safe with me. That much I can promise. But there may be others, sometimes—" His expression seemed to darken. "I may really have to, you know."

"Don't tell me, like, if your country calls—or something like that?"

"All right," he said abruptly. "Enough of that. Let's finish our wine and get out of here. It's a pretty day. At least we can spend a little time together before you have to get back to Jerry."

"Not more than an hour. And then no more. Not while Jerry's here. I owe him that much, don't you think?"

"Sure. I'll stay out of the picture until he goes back to New York. That's only fair." He pointed up in the direction of the *Hôtel des Invalides*. "But right now, we can just walk around, maybe go look at Napoleon's caskets. All nine of them."

She laughed. "As long as we stay away from the eighth arrondissement, and the first. And the *Avenue Montaigne*."

"All the fashion centers."

"Right. And the *Rue Chabon*. And the *Jeu de Paume*."

"I get it. Where anyone can recognize you."

"It's been great, being a private person. For these few weeks, anyway."

"Okay. Okay. We'll stay away from any street where you are known. I wouldn't want anything bad to happen to you in Paris."

"Oh, Sam. Nothing bad can ever happen in Paris."

They smiled at each other. If only that could be so.

Chapter Twenty-eight

It was late afternoon, almost four thirty, and Jerry was still sleeping when she let herself into the apartment, but he stirred as she shut the door behind her.

"I tried to be quiet," she said. "I didn't want to wake you."

"That's okay," he said. "I had a good rest." He smiled at her, a sleepy, satisfied sort of smile. "Come on over here." She put her bag and her jacket onto a chair and sat down next to him on the bed. He reached up and drew her down so he could kiss her. "Thanks for letting me sleep. I was bushed."

"Do you need to go back to sleep?"

"No. I need to eat. I'm starved. Never got dinner last night and then nothing but some pretzels on the plane. That sick kid next to me kind of took away my appetite. And just a coffee this morning." He looked at his watch, on the table next to the bed. "We can go get an early dinner."

She smiled at him. "The French don't eat an early dinner." She was glad, actually. She preferred to say what she had to in a public place. Jerry would never make a scene in front of strangers. Nor, for that matter, in front of friends. But alone, she might have to contend with a very angry man.

"So we'll just be boorish American tourists and I'm sure they'll put up with us. We'll find something, a sandwich or something, and we won't call it dinner." He pulled back the covers and got out of bed. "Give me a minute to get dressed."

He had slept naked and Marge had to admit, he was in awfully good shape.

Don't I have a nice-looking boyfriend? she asked herself. *Even with his hair all mussed up. He does have nice hair, thick and nice to get your hands into.*

She realized she was looking for ways to add pluses to the "Jerry" column.

"How long will you be able to stay?" she called to him in the bathroom.

"Gotta be back by Monday," he called back. "That tax fraud case I told you about."

"So we have three days."

"Right. Anything special you want to do while I'm here? How about the flea market?"

"Not the *Puce*. I'd be sure to run into someone there. But I've never been to the Asian community. I hear it's a great place to pick up treasures. In the thirteenth."

"We could go to Disneyland Paris. Spend the day. We could do that tomorrow."

She was eager to please him. "Sure. That would be fun."

He came out of the bathroom. She laughed. "You need a shave."

"Yeah. Well I didn't think to bring a razor. And I don't want to use Mack's."

"Never mind. You look cute. Sexy."

He handed her her bag and her jacket. "Hold that thought," he said. "Right now, I just want to eat."

* * * *

She waited till he'd finished his beef bourguignon and was on his second glass of the good Bordeaux he'd ordered.

"Are you feeling good? Nicely fed?" she asked.

"You bet. Why?"

"Because I have to tell you what you may not want to hear."

"Now what? More about Sam?"

"Yes. More about Sam."

"Oh, damn, Marge. You're ruining my dinner."

"I know. I'm sorry."

"Okay. What is it?"

"I had nothing to do with it"— she crossed her fingers under the table; that was sort of true—"but it turns out Sam is here. In Paris."

"I'll be damned! Am I going to have to fight that guy? I mean, toe to toe? Out in the alley? Behind the school? Jesus, Marge!"

"It's not like that. He wants to be with me. He has the right to go anywhere in the world he wants to, you know. It's not like either one of you asked the other's permission. And for sure, no one asked me!"

"Are you defending him?"

"Come on, Jerry. It's not like that."

"Yeah? Well, I feel like this city is getting too small for the two of us. Or the three of us."

"I've never seen you like this, Jerry."

"Like what? Mad?"

"Jealous. And unreasonable."

"I'm never unreasonable. You know that much about me. But I'm plenty jealous." He paused, getting control of himself. "You bet I'm jealous. We've been together all these years, you and I, and I thought we had at least a comfortable relationship. And some guy out of your past—your *high school* past, for Christ's sake!—suddenly shows up, and like that! I'm turned into a potted plant in the corner. How do you think I feel?"

Oh, dear. Marge did the worst thing she could have done. She laughed!

"You're not a potted plant, Jerry. You could never be a potted plant."

He was turning red. It was not a pretty sight, and she was instantly sorry.

"I'm sorry, Jerry," she said. "I shouldn't have laughed. But this whole thing is so ridiculous."

"Ridiculous? A guy beats my ass in court and then it turns out he's also screwing my girl?"

Now it was Marge's turn to get mad.

"Number one, Jerry. I'm not your girl. You don't own me. And Sam isn't screwing me. I told you nothing happened. How dare you!? And what's more, you said you did okay in court. He didn't 'beat your ass.'"

"All right. I'm sorry." He didn't sound sorry. "It was a figure of speech. Sort of. But I feel like a lot's been going on behind my back and I don't like it."

They glared at each other for a while. A long while. Then Jerry said, "Let's get out of here."

Marge said nothing, but stood up. She waited while he paid the bill. They left silently.

They'd walked about a block, and Jerry said, "Where is he?"

"What do you mean?"

"He's here in Paris. He's staying somewhere. You must know where."

"Why? What are you going to do?"

"I'm going to do the civilized thing. I'm going to talk to him."

She thought for a while as they walked a little farther.

"Okay. I'll tell you. That's fair."

And she gave him the name of the hotel on the corner of the *Rue Grenelle* and the *Place des Invalides.*

"It's still early," he said. "I'm going there now. Where will you be?"

"I'll go into that café where we met this morning. I never got to read my paper. And Jerry"—she put her hand on his arm as she realized she really was very fond of him—"don't fight. Remember, you're both good guys."

He looked long and hard at her, and she saw that he'd calmed down. "You know I love you, Marge. You're precious to me and I'd do anything to keep you. I will fight, but it will be a fair fight and a civilized one, I promise." And right there on the street, with people walking around them, he held her close and kissed her long and tenderly. And, this being Paris, no one paid any attention to them.

Chapter Twenty-nine

What a blessing it is that it's possible to sit in a café in Paris for hours and hours, drinking a single cup of coffee, and no one shoos you out. A couple of hours passed while Marge read her paper, and also read part of a book she'd downloaded into her smart phone. She was also left alone to go through all sorts of moods and worries and scenarios while she waited to find out what was happening between the two men.

When at last Jerry came in, she searched his face for a clue. He looked grim, but he didn't look mad at her. That was a good sign.

The waiter came over and Jerry ordered a coffee.

She didn't need to ask anything. Her face said clearly she was eager to hear his report.

"Well," Jerry said, "lawyer to lawyer, Sam Packard could give a clinic in how to do effective oral argument. He managed to convince me."

"Convince you of what?"

"He wasn't so crass about it, but bottom line, I've had you for six years, and he should have a chance to spend some quality time with you to make his case. Like if I said no, I was being a scaredy-cat. I'm not quite sure how he did it."

"For God's sake, I don't know whether to laugh or be furious. I feel like a hunk of cheese, being passed around for everyone to take a slice. You two are such—such—*men!*"

"I know. I'm sorry."

"And 'scaredy-cat'? What are you two? Ten?"

"Well, that isn't exactly what was said." His coffee arrived and he stopped to unwrap and stir a tiny sugar cube into it. "It was more like 'a real man stands up and doesn't run away from the challenge. And is man enough to live with the result.' Something like that. Anyway, I decided I don't want to be around while he has a chance to spread his feathers and see if you like the display."

"You mean like a peacock?"

"Yeah. I think that's what I mean."

"So what are you going to do?"

"Well, remember, I didn't even bring a toothbrush. So I'm going to just ride out to Orly and get the next plane back to New York. And I'm going to trust that you're a sensible and honorable woman, and you'll do the right thing and not let yourself get swept off your feet. And that I'll have the backbone to accept your choice if it's not in my favor. Thumbs up or thumbs down. Like they did with the gladiators long ago."

How funny. Gladiators. Like at Carnuntum.

He sat back in his chair and drank his coffee and looked long and hard and so lovingly at her face, as though he'd need to keep the memory forever.

He surely didn't know it, but Marge felt closer to him then than she ever had in their six, almost seven years together.

He finished his coffee. He stood up. He leaned down and kissed her.

"I love you Marge," he said. And she watched him disappear out onto the *Rue Grenelle*. He was flagging down a taxi to take him to Orly so he could fly back to New York. She hoped he'd have a good flight and that there'd be no sick kids anywhere near him.

Chapter Thirty

Her phone pinged at her and she saw that she had a message from Sam.

Has he left? Can you talk?

Can I see you?

I need a rest from u guys.

Let's have breakfast. 9a.m.

Good idea. Fresh start. Luxembourg Gardens?

At the playground? We can watch the kids.

That brings back a memory.

I knew you'd remember.

I'll bring coffee and croissants.

:-)

She put the phone away.

Yes, a fresh start. It's what we needed.

Back at the apartment, she took a long, luxurious bath, deliberately thought about nothing important, and had a good night's sleep.

* * * *

She woke to a glorious morning. Paris was all sunshine and bluebirds and good omens. A lovely autumn day, not too cold, and crisp with promise. The *Jardin du Luxembourg* was lovely, as it always is, and Sam could not have suggested a better place to start their day together.

He was waiting at one of the flimsy metal tables near the playground, where the bird-chirpy trill of children already brightened the morning. He had a Thermos in front of him and a bag of croissants at the ready.

"The hotel packed them up for me," he said, offering the bag to her as she sat down.

She took a croissant out of the bag and her fingers were instantly buttery. He handed her a paper napkin.

"Mmm." She took a bite. "Perfect," she said. "Thanks."

He poured a mug of coffee for her.

And then they sat, just smiling at each other.

Then he reached over and put his hands over hers.

"This is much better," he said. "We've cleared the air. No secrets."

"I know. Jerry's mad, but it's better this way."

"I'll say this, Marge. He's mad, of course, but he is a grown-up and took it as well as he could, in the circumstance. And now, may the best man win, and let's not talk about Jerry any more. At least for the time being." Marge nodded her agreement. The subject was closed. For the time being.

Marge turned to watch the children. "I love that you suggested meeting here. It's been ages since I thought about that afternoon we spent together."

"At the little after-school playground near the day care center."

"Watching the children."

The memory seemed to light up the eyes of each of them.

"You were so funny," Marge said. "You were imagining the futures of each kid. Like the one who'd grow up to be a fussy little male busybody. You thought he'd be a news commentator on TV. And which one a nagging housewife. You picked one to be a stand-up comedian, and another would be a bank robber."

"And the mothers," Sam said. "You got mad at one mom because she was really scolding her kid for getting his shirt dirty. I had to keep you from running over there and getting into a fight with her." Sam laughed.

"You were kind of a handful in those days, Marge. Full of piss and vinegar. No, I shouldn't call it that. You were full of ginger. Just the liveliest, most eager-for-life kid I'd ever known. Male or female."

"You didn't mind, did you?"

"Mind? Marge, I wanted you so badly, there were plenty of nights I couldn't even sleep, thinking about you. Imagining our life together. And then, that night of the prom, the stupid dumb fight we got into, I was so mad at myself, I practically wrecked the car driving home. And then, that summer, when you didn't answer my letters, well, I wasn't fit to live with for many months. But I finally managed to tell myself to forget you. I said, 'She was just your first love. There'll be others.' And I got on with my life. College, law school, the military. I did well at all of that, and it was all so I could forget you."

"You're leaving out a lot."

"It doesn't matter now. You're sitting here with me now, it's an absolutely spectacular day," he waved a hand taking it all in, the park, the children, the cloudless skies above, "and I'm the luckiest man in the whole, wide world." He said those last words slowly, savoring each one. "The very luckiest." And then he smiled at her. "And you are absolutely the most beautiful woman in the whole, wide world. And those are the last serious words I'm speaking today. From here on, the day is just for fun." He turned and looked at the children. "God, they're sweet, aren't they? They haven't a clue what lies ahead. Look at that kid," he said. He pointed at a very little girl who was twirling around and around, arms outstretched, making herself dizzy. "That one's going to be an astronaut."

Marge laughed. "Good choice. And that one, over there, the little boy trying to get the whole pile of blocks away from the other one, he's going to be a hedge fund manager."

And so they played their game until they'd finished all the coffee in the Thermos and eaten all the croissants in the bag. Sam crumpled up the paper bag and took it to a nearby trash receptacle. Marge said her shoulder bag was big enough to hold the Thermos, and she stowed it away in her big Gucci bag. They took one last, long look at the children and then started a slow stroll through the Gardens. They stopped to watch some old men playing *pétanque*, old men in baggy corduroy pants and baggy sweaters, having a great time, tossing the hard little balls across the dirt playing area.

"I never did figure out the rules of that game," Sam said. "But that's going to be me, some day. I'll be here in Paris, in my baggy old clothes, a baggy old man myself, playing what looks to me like the simplest game that was ever invented. Probably by then that's all I'll be able to do."

"You expect to be a cranky old codger?"

"Absolutely."

They both laughed. They both knew there was no way that was going to be true.

"And you?" he said. "What are you going to be?"

"I'm going to be a grand old lady, very elegant, and very rich. I'll have tossed tons of lovers aside and I'll have a history so fascinating, they'll be writing biographies of my life."

He stopped her, right there on the path alongside the *pétanque* ground, and he said, "No, Marge." He put his arms around her and held her close. "No life of lovers tossed aside. Only one lover, only one. Forever." There was a glitter in his eyes that looked like a fire deep inside and suddenly Marge knew they were about to cross a threshold.

"You said 'nothing serious' Sam. Remember?"

She felt a tremor that went through his body, and she remembered that warm current, the first time their bodies touched, so long ago, in the cafeteria of their high school.

"The hell with that," he said. "Let's get out of here. Let's get back to the hotel. Now."

And in that moment, Marge Webster, grown-up woman, powerful executive and industry driver, figure of legendary independence and drive, practically a force of nature, was ready to go anywhere with Sam Packard, anywhere in the world he wanted to go.

Can't help it. I just can't help it.

They were near a taxi stand, outside the Luxembourg. In ten minutes, ten excruciating minutes in the back seat of the taxi, they were at his hotel, through the lobby, and into his room.

* * * *

The next minutes could not be counted. Time disappeared as they managed, somehow—so clumsy in their eagerness—to get each other's clothes off, to get their bodies onto the bed, to bring together mouths and hands and every inch of skin, as though to make one person out of two, to let all the years slip away and be again young, hungry animals filled with the discovery of their passion for each other.

Was it all a few minutes? Or had hours passed?

The room, with the curtains still drawn since that morning against the light, was dimly lit. They lay tangled up together, exhausted, bedclothes every which way, pillows on the floor. Hearts pounding. Sam got himself up on one elbow and looked down at Marge. He seemed to be marveling at the very fact that she was there, in his bed. His few whispered words were simple.

"I am so much in love with you."

She closed her eyes and pulled him down close to her. They kissed, and right there, in the corner of her mouth, she felt his tongue touch that very spot that belonged to him.

* * * *

It was hours later that Sam left the bed, walked to the window, drew back the curtain and saw that it was nighttime. He turned to Marge, who had pulled a sheet around her.

"Are you hungry?" he asked.

"What?"

He laughed. "I mean for dinner?"

"Oh." She laughed, too. "I guess. I hadn't thought about food."

"Should we go out or call room service?"

"I don't care."

"Will you stay here with me tonight?"

"I'd like to."

"We can go back in the morning to your place if there's anything you need."

"Some clean clothes, I guess."

And that's how they managed the next days—back and forth between the two places, taking only what they needed. Sam charmed Mme. Pilard with his good French, and she made it clear to him that she approved of him and not "that other one."

They spent their days walking and walking and walking around the city, exploring all the places where no one in the fashion industry, no media person, and no one who had ever worked with Marge was likely to recognize her. They stayed mostly to the outer arrondissements, where they discovered wonderful bakeries and local jazz spots and Asian and African and Middle Eastern neighborhoods, tiny thrift shops and local galleries and everywhere, beautiful architecture and two-hundred-year-old city streets where two-thousand-year-old paths used to run. They sat in out-of-the way cafés, inside to talk and outside to people-watch. They fantasized the private lives of passersby and made up names for them. They went to the *Père Lachaise* cemetery and marveled together that it held the graves of countless world-renowned artists, writers, movie stars, politicians, so many that they needed to buy a printed set of pages, available at a little nearby shop, to help them find even a small number of them—too many for a single afternoon.

And at night, he held her in his arms and told her that he'd always known she was the most extraordinary woman in the entire world, and that these hours in bed proved it.

He was a happy man.

And Marge was happy, too.

Chapter Thirty-one

And then it was time to go home. Sam got a message from his office that he was needed there, and Marge knew these fantasy days had to end, that she was quite strong and healthy, and ready to get back to work. They agreed to travel separately. Sam was needed immediately but Marge needed to close up Bridey's place and alert her staff that she was fine and was on her way home. She let Gena Shaw know that a full presentation of everything she'd missed and everything that was planned needed to be ready in three days, and if the mice had been playing while the cat was away, now was the time to hide the cheese and get everything ready for inspection.

Gena's message came back.

> *Can't wait 2 c u.*

> *We missed u, but yr systems worked well, the*
> *"class president" kept order in yr absence, and*
> *now "the teacher" can take over again. No harm*
> *done. LOL c u soon*

Back in New York, her first call was to Bridey. Who greeted her with, "I want to hear every word. Your call was so mysterious. Tell me. Tell me everything."

"Too much for a phone call. I need to shower and make a couple of calls. I won't be expected back at the office for another couple of days, but I have plenty to do in the meantime. I have an appointment to see Dr. Diaz uptown. She said she wants to see me when I get back, be sure I'm ready to go back to work. Can you meet me at the place over on the Upper

West Side? The one up by Columbia. It's quiet and we can talk. And no one knows me up there."

"Why do you have to be where no one knows you? You should be used to being a celebrity by now. Plenty of people on the Upper West Side know me—from the cooking show. I don't mind. It's good for ratings."

Marge laughed. "I guess that says something about the demographics of our markets. Yours is up by the university, where people cook. Mine is the Upper East Side and the Garment District." She paused for a minute to think about that. "Anyway, I think I got used to hiding while I was away. I kind of liked it."

"Well, it's time to come out of the closet. When should we meet?"

"Right away. No, soon. I can be there in forty minutes. Can you get away?"

"Mack is here. He'll watch the kids. See you in forty."

* * * *

She ordered a hamburger and sweet potato fries. And a glass of red wine. Bridey had coffee.

"Where to start? There's so much."

"Start at the beginning."

"You were there at the beginning. It started in high school. You know that part. You know that Sam and I go back that far."

"So that's what this is about. Sam Packard."

"Right. And you can stop leering at me. This is serious."

"Okay, honey. I won't leer. What happened while you were in Paris?"

"It wasn't Paris. Well, it was Paris, too, but it was before Paris."

"You called that you needed the place in Paris so I figured—"

So Marge filled her in. She told her about Sam tracking her down in London.

"Everywhere I went, there he was. He came over twice while I was in London. And oh, Bridey, he was wonderful. Sam Packard is really wonderful."

Bridey looked at her friend with that expression that asks the question only a good friend is allowed to ask. "And did you— you know—?"

"I would have. Would I ever have."

"But—?"

"A divine providence intervened. It was funny, actually. But that's not the story." She went on to tell the rest, about her determination to keep Sam away so she could think, and about Vienna, the mysterious Christiane

Riemer, and the children in the playground chattering in German, and the sweet little toddler with the round cheeks who waved his bye-bye at her. "Bridey, that little boy looked into my eyes as though he had a message he really wanted me to hear, only he hadn't any words yet. And for the first time, it broke my heart that I have no children."

Bridey looked at her friend lovingly. "I think you will, Marge. I really think you will."

"Well, let me go on. You may be right."

"Oh?!"

"Oh, no! I didn't mean—Oh, no. Heavens! No, let me go on."

And she told her the rest. How Sam waited till he and Jerry didn't need to see each other in court anymore, and how he then went to him and told him everything and how Jerry showed up in Paris, and Sam showed up in Paris, and they duked it out in their lawyerly way and Jerry left her alone in Paris with Sam. "And that's the whole story."

"Not exactly. That's not exactly the whole story."

"What do you mean? It is. That's everything."

"Are you kidding? Look at you. You look great. You're glowing, and it's not the extra couple of pounds you've put on. Marge, you look happy. You look happier than I've seen you in years. You look happier than you did the day *Lady Fair* took the lead in circulation figures *and* ad revenues for all fashion periodicals, worldwide. You look happier than the day you broke two stories, the 'two scoops in one' issue—the Sonny Gaile wedding *and* the Romy deVere revelations. You look as happy as a teenager with her first love. That's it. That's what it is. You have the glow of puppy love about you. Hot damn, Marge! You are well and truly in love with Sam Packard, aren't you? You're goofy about him now, as much as you were goofy in love when you were a freshman in love with the most popular senior boy."

"But it's crazy, Bridey. Isn't it? But still, he's adorable. And he's funny and sweet. And he's smart. He's very, *very* smart. And I feel like a teenager again."

"And in bed?"

Marge just raised her eyes, as though to heaven. And shook her head, to say there were no words.

"That good, huh?"

Marge nodded. And sighed. The memory alone took her breath away.

"Well," Bridey said. "That's tough competition. What does Sam want?"

"To hear him, I am the moon and the stars, and all he wants is me and he'll do whatever I want." She paused. "He'd go, if I sent him away, but he wouldn't go easily. I know that."

"I get it. With sex that good, you're not about to send him away."

"It's not about the sex. It's how he makes me feel."

"And that is—?"

"He makes me happy. Bridey, I don't know how else to say it. He makes me happy."

"Oh, dear. I think you're right. You definitely look happy. But then, there's Jerry."

"Right."

"Who you've been with for a long time—"

"More than six years—"

"And who's a good guy and this will break his heart."

"Yes. If it hasn't already. He's being a good scout about it, but it hurts. I know."

"I'm sure you've asked yourself if this is one of those fling-type things, like at a summer resort or a Caribbean cruise, where it's all fantasy and after a little while, it peters out and that's all it was, just a fling."

"Of course I have." Bridey saw her friend's expression change, in an odd way. As though she was letting something peel away and letting Bridey see into a part of her soul that she'd always kept to herself. "Bridey, life with Jerry would not be bad. Like we always say about him, he's a good guy. Any woman would make a good choice to marry Jerry. But I'm not any woman. I never was. I'm not an ordinary person. You've known me forever. You, of all people, know that's true. I've been odd, and weird, and driven, and super-focused, ever since I was a little girl. I didn't get to be at the top of *Lady Fair* by being ordinary.

"And Sam is not ordinary. There are levels to him that make him very special—and maybe mysterious. Not bad, I think. But special. Definitely not ordinary. I think there are things about him that I'll never know." She paused and put her fingertip to the corner of her mouth. But she wasn't going to tell Bridey about that. She went on. "So he's a good fit for me. Much better than Jerry. I like Jerry. He's okay. But he's just okay. That's why I never married him. That's why he never made me happy. He never made me sad or angry. He just never made me happy. I didn't realize it until I was with Sam. Sam puts me together, the weird, wild kid I was along with the very special adult woman I am. Sam is like that, too. Adult in a way most men can't be, tough and strong and capable in interesting, mysterious ways that maybe I'll get to understand and maybe I won't. And he can still be a kid, a little boy, a very unordinary person. And I'm happy with him—because we fit together."

Bridey looked at her friend long and hard. She knew she was seeing into a deeper layer of Marge's soul than had ever been exposed to her before. But it was a layer she'd always understood was there. It was what had attracted her all those years ago and made her glad to be Marge's friend.

"You're right, Marge. I understand, and I wouldn't try to argue you out of it. I don't know if you and Jerry can be friends after this. Probably not. But Mack and I, we can go on as his friends, if he wants to. And I know you won't mind."

"Of course not. Who knows? He and Sam may need to meet up in court again in the future, and they'll be just fine. They know how to be grown-ups."

Bridey laughed. "Not like the girls. Remember how you described it: *'I hate her guts. I'll never talk to her again.'*"

"Exactly." Yes, they'd had that conversation, months ago. "I wish girls could learn to shake hands and be over it. But I guess they don't feel strong enough." She ate up the last of her fries. "Anyway, I've got to go now. Gotta talk to Jerry. Gotta talk to Sam."

"I need to get home, too. Mack has had the kids since this morning. He's probably ready for a break by now. And I've got recipes to test."

"I'll be in the office on Monday. Come in and we'll talk about some ideas I have."

They went out onto Broadway, air-kissed, and hailed separate cabs, Marge to go uptown and Bridey to go back home, across town.

Chapter Thirty-two

"How did he take it?"

"I think he already knew. I think he knew when he left Paris. I think he knew before I did."

Sam smiled at her and brushed a curl back from her forehead. "Was it so hard for you to know? To decide about me, I mean?"

She was in his arms and in his bed, and soon the lights would be out and they would no longer be thinking about anything at all, because they'd be among the moon and the stars, in the world of fire and ice, and the ordinary world would have disappeared for a while.

He ran the tip of his tongue across her lower lip where a drop of duck sauce lingered from the take-in food they'd ordered.

She returned the kiss. "You're a sly one, Sam Packard, but you're not catching me in that trap. You know perfectly well, it was easy to love you." Again, she kissed him, lightly. "I've always loved you." And again, another light kiss. "But it was hard to hurt Jerry. And he was hurt, he really was. It came out of the blue, no warning at all. Within twenty-four hours, a relationship of years was taken away from him. And it was done by a man he knew only as a courtroom opponent, so it was a professional blow as well as a personal one. Of course it hurt him. And of course it was hard for me to do that to him."

"Okay, that's a very pretty speech. But I saw his face the very first night, when he came out of the courtroom and saw us talking there in the corridor. He knew something was up."

"I wasn't so sure."

"Well, there you are, darling. You don't have the thousand-eyes vision that I have."

"Like a house fly?"

"Right." He laughed. "Like a house fly." He reached across her to turn off the light, leaving the room only dimly lit by a small lamp that had been left on in the living room. His naked body was across hers and she looked so lovely, looking up at him from the pillow, he had to kiss her. "You know, there have to be *some* things I can do that you can't."

"Oh?"

"Of course. So we can tell the boys from the girls."

"Name one."

"I can pee standing up."

"Really? Well, so can I."

"Oh?"

"And what's more, I can do it no hands."

He had to laugh. "Shut up, dear," he said, kissing her again. "No man likes a smart dame."

"I know."

"Here. Let me show you something I know you can't do."

And they both shut up, because there were no words for the slow, patient exploration he made of her body, of all her senses, and her capacity for deep, primal, exquisite responses. There were no words, and there was no passage of time, because he took her to where time begins and ends and the world is created and the world ends and there are stars and fire and oceans rise and fall.

And then, after a while, after she had done the same for him, he whispered the only words that would be heard that night.

"My God, Marge. I am so much in love with you."

And they rested and were quiet in each other's arms.

About the Author

Joan Myra Bronston grew up in New York City, married her college sweetheart, and went with him to Germany for a year while he was in the Army and where she worked as a telex operator and mail clerk. They then moved to Austria where Joan spent five years teaching at an international school. She is the mother of three wonderful girls and the grandmother of a super-wonderful grandson. Joan was also a secretary, social investigator, and psychiatric researcher, before entering law school and eventually becoming a corporate attorney. In addition to her years in Europe, Joan has lived in Pittsburgh, Chicago, and, for 18 years, Salt Lake City. At last, she has closed the circle and returned to her first and most beloved—New York City. Visit her website at jmbronston.com, find her on Facebook, and follow her on Twitter @JMBronston.